AND DEATH DREAM US ALL

A Story of Love, Obsession & Hysteria

To Staci and To the Shadows

Often, the monsters who invade our dreams are merely obscure reflections of that within ourselves which we fear, so blow out the candle and fear not, your shadow is there to embrace you, for it is the one who truly knows you.

Cheryl Anne Gardner

AND DEATH DREAMT US ALL

A Story of Love, Obsession & Hysteria

A

Twisted Knickers Publication

YOU LEFT IT THERE…
> Cast it away on the side of the road,
> An oil smudge upon the pavement,
> Filthy viscous thing that it was.
> Dead thing.
> Evil thing.
> Old.
> Desiccated.
> And you left it there.
> Walked away,
> Once and for all.

1

Duty Calls

April 10, 1998

I t was five in the morning. Too damn early to look at a dead body, but there I was, arrived at the cottage, and there it was, leaning hard against the horizon, low in the shadows as the first hint of dawn was just barely beginning to break through the tangle of clouds and tree branches. Covered in what looked like efflorescent blue-green sludge, it appeared as if the place had long since belched out its last dying breath, leaving its decayed carcass to ooze a lifetime of bile from its mortared pores. These ransacked and forgotten country cottages are safe havens for all manner of repugnant creatures. The demons of the twilight. Cannibals. Shape-shifters. Illusionists.

Chipped asphalt and dirty fog caught between my clenched teeth, I felt like I'd been held hostage for hours by the dismal winding roads and the dense countryside. It had taken the better part of the morning to get to this god-forsaken place. I didn't think my car was going to make it, coughing and sputtering in protest, but there I was, all back-wooded, nowhere in respect to the civilized world, and the better part of the drive spent in quiet contemplation hadn't done a single thing to improve my mood, either. All it had done was force the dread closer to the surface. I could skim my tongue across it as it clung coldly to my upper lip.

Leaning half detached from its frame, a gigantic slab of rotted wood — allegedly the front door — was open, and so I walked across the threshold. The cold bit into my legs and lower back as I entered, and my knees felt like the remnants of the rusted iron hinges that lay in the dried leaves at my feet. I nudged them with my toe, but there wasn't a glimmer of hope left in them. At one time, this cottage had been a summer retreat perhaps, charming and quaint in its better days, I imagined, but it didn't take more than a few footsteps into the main room before all the lovely things I had imagined left my thoughts forever. Shabby and outworn, this cottage was now just an insignificant oversight, one that should have been razed to the ground a century ago.

Looking around quickly for my liaison, I took a few deliberate mental notes. Two notes to be exact: filth and vermin. What I saw wasn't pretty, and so I didn't have to imagine the ruin that plagued this place. The interior hadn't held up much better than the exterior. The room reeked of animal urine and excrement — a foul latrine for wandering savages and beasts — and there was an eerie sense of movement beneath my feet, like the building was crumbling and shifting around me, each step I took a reminder that the irrefutable agents of time would eventually claw its very foundation apart, starting with the ceiling, which had caved in, exposing blackened beams, greasy and charred from burning candles, incense, and uncontained fires. Stifling and suffocating odors clung to the congested air, and the walls, what was left of them, had receded into the murk, as the paint had lost all its will and tenacity, coming loose from the plaster in humiliating defeat.

Mold and death lurked behind every fleck of chipped paint. Mold and death, tended by legions of unseen parasitic creatures, moving outward from the blackness — consuming — until this hideous place and all its history would exist no more.

It made me wonder. *A fresh coat of paint?* It's amazing what a fresh coat of paint can do. Maybe a fresh coat of skin might make the mangled meat pile in the next room appear more human. *Or maybe not.* I hadn't seen the victim yet and wasn't sure I wanted to. I've always hated that word: Victim. No other word affirms the tenuous relationship we have with vice and virtue, but anyway, there was too much to see here. The ruminations of a thousand derelicts were scrawled across the walls in what looked like blood and feces, but a quick glance was all I could manage before a shiver of something unnatural rushed against my back and shoulders. The cold of it digging into my bones. I could say it was just an artifact — space, time, the sun's trajectory — but it wasn't. It was a shadow, come for me, and it took its time, slipping into the daylight from a distance. As if in no particular hurry, it seemed to meander its way across the wall. Seemed to turn and look directly at me without concern as it settled itself into the sweating void of plaster and paint.

I felt it presence … Felt its eyes on me … Felt the room begin to swell against its boundaries, and then all sound stopped, neither a breath of wind through the trees nor the rustle of a fallen leaf against the eaves. I was alone in the room, and terror was closing in. I could taste the metal in my teeth, but I held fast to my position even as I felt the shadow's gaze slip over me. I clenched my fists, and it just laughed at me. Laughed at my sweaty-palmed resolve, then it flexed its shoulders once, twice, and the measure of its fingers began to extend slowly, sinking almost to the floorboards. They twitched like the legs of a spider, scritch, scratch, scratching, as if it were making a mad attempt to rip the floor out from under my feet, so I remained still, unable to move or breathe. Then out of nowhere, upon wings made of whisper, a raven, large and scraggy, soared through the open door. It flew over my head, and then, stretching out its claws, it took perch upon the shadow's shoulder. It squawked. Turned towards me. Glared at me with blood-red demonic eyes. It was taunting me. The goddamn repulsive creature just taunted me with raised wings and angry stamping talons, chastising me for some concealed sin. A sin that I had long refused to acknowledge let alone come to grips with.

It wasn't my fault.

I wanted to say it out loud, my confession, slathered in guilt and a whimper. The words almost fell from my lips … almost … but I choked them back along with my fear. When I opened my eyes, the shadow and its loyal familiar had vanished, melted into obscurity, now nothing more than a mere inkblot amongst the many other stains on the wall.

"Rowan!"

My eyes fell blurry back into the gloom, and instantly, the room was bustling with people again. Uniformed officers trudged about, taking notes, speaking to each other in hushed voices, carefully gathering evidence, and Inspector Reed stood beside me, gently resting his immense hairy club of a hand on my shoulder, his pockmarked face flushed and dripping with sweat. "You seemed lost there, lass," he said more as a statement of fact than a question, but the words just slid right by me. "Come on now, Rowan. You might want to load up. We should have the markers out for you shortly. It's in the next room."

"Yes, Inspector," was all I could manage in response. My bland tone was in no way indicative of any personal feelings that I might have held for Inspector Reed. I prefer to keep my emotions in check while on a job. I actually like Inspector Reed, like him a lot, but his physical presence, well, it's just overwhelming. Too much aftershave, too much of what he ate for breakfast lingering on his breath. He placed a cigarette to his lips, lit it, and then sucked in deeply, releasing a cloud of stale breath and smoke in a wheeze. "You know what I like best about you, Rowan? Don't worry, you can put that blank I-don't-give-a-shit look away because I'm just going to tell you. You are a woman of few words. Just don't need them, I suppose?"

"No, I suppose I don't," was my only less-than-slightly-blank reply, and at least we agreed on something.

In spite of his unseemly presence, Inspector Reed was a kind and decent man, a man you had no choice but to like. I knew this simply because of the way he forced a rather crude and misshapen smile at me. He left in his wake a long and distinguished career, mostly due to that smile. Words rarely escaped him. He was just respectfully spare with them, but he was never spare with that smile. It happens often that homicide Inspectors tend to lose the ability even to force a smile. Usually within the first year. I have heard it said that a kind of numbness takes over. Emotions wane and the intensity of focus increases exponentially. For some. Only the ones who were born to be witnesses survive. Certain defense mechanisms instinctual to the breed kick in and take over. For others not fortunate enough, not built strong enough, well, they suffer and go mad, departing after a year or so for employment better suited to their more fragile sensibilities. Security men or traffic wardens, perhaps. Reed is tops on a very short list, so I had to admire his cold candor and his matter-of-fact demeanor. The strength of his presence was comforting to me right then, and maybe it was his authoritarian goodness that sent the shadow crawling back to the mists of oblivion.

I needed to believe that, and so I did.

"It's a bad one today, bloody fuckin' mess, it is. Goddamn it's hot in here," he coughed out in a rasp as he took a rag from his pocket and scraped the stale sweat from his brow. "Just stay focused and do your magic, Rowan."

"Yes, Inspector, of course."

I pled a weak smile back at him while giving him a

sympathetic nod, and then I adjusted the camera strap, which had now begun digging into my neck. He gave me a comfort pat on the shoulder and then pointed in the direction of a doorway, a darkened hollow, leading to what I was certain was probably a gateway straight to hell.

While taking care not to disturb anything that might be construed as evidence, I took slow and measured steps, Reed following behind me as silent as a raptor in an updraft. The corridor was long. Dark and dank. The floorboards squealed in agony with every footfall, and the threadbare carpet runner, no more than a frayed rag presenting refuge to an entire civilization of who knows what, did not help muffle the reluctant echo of our approach. Even the smug and snarly cockroaches mocked us with their insolence as they scuttled over our shoes. Every step seemed like slow damnation, but remarkably, the corridor that had seemed endless only a moment before did, in fact, do just that. We reached the door, and without hesitation, I opened it and went in.

I don't really know what I was expecting. I try not to have expectations. I try to keep my mind clear. I need to see, really see, and that is just not possible with expectations. However, expectations aside, I wasn't ready for the room. It was alive with death. That's the best I can do to describe it.

Massive shapes, covered in debris, loomed ominously in the heavy gloom. A rusted iron bedstead held a precarious and haunting position in the corner of the room, and a dull glow offering the only light, strained its way through the depressing, dust-laden rags that had once been used to shade the windows from prying eyes.

The light, meager as it was, was better than the darkness. Death lingered in the darkness like a virulent fiend, waiting, patiently waiting to extract the life and light out of anything that happened to wander foolishly into its domain. I was just such a fool, and as I moved further into the room, I could hear the slow and monotonous drip of a tap coming from somewhere off to my left. *How could this place still have running water?* A well perhaps. A haunted well in the middle of the forest. What nonsense, a dripping tap was the least of my concerns and completely out of my visual range. *Focus Rowan, don't think, just focus.* But as much as I would have liked to will myself to do it, I couldn't focus. Couldn't think. Couldn't speak. Couldn't help myself. *Fool, fool, fool, stark raving mad fool.* I was a fool, had always been. I never felt as strong as I wanted to be, pretended to be, and suddenly, I started to shake uncontrollably. My entire body felt as if it had succumbed to some sort of seizure, so I thrust a bit of honest Inspector logic into it. I suppose, in some slight way, I feared the bloody image before me, and yet, even the disconcerting spasms of my body couldn't compel me to look away. Never am I able to look away. My fear doesn't hinder me in the way it does for most people, for it's not fear the average person can sympathize with. It's not bravery. I just have no fight or flight response, not one that could make rational assumptions, let alone decisions, anyway. It's not morbid curiosity, either. It's morbid intellectual interest. I'm searching, always searching for death's great metaphor. So I pushed my hair out of my face and took a deep breath. I might be a fool, but I am in control. This is how I work: cold, calm, and unhurried.

SNAP!

"Jesus, Reed."

"What? What do you see, Rowan?"

"Hell hath no mercy."

"What?"

"What do you mean what? I meant exactly that, Reed. No Mercy. It's a fucking cliché." SNAP! "But if you need it in plain English, I see too much blood."

Tossed like a sack of rags and rocks, the body lay on the floor in the center of the room, splayed out in a mangled slapdash sort of way on a stained and shredded mattress, her hair snagged and tangled about the twisted, displaced bedsprings. A black silk slip lay thrown over her head, concealing her face, and the remnants of a garrote remained embedded in her neck so deeply that the enraged, lacerated flesh had wedded itself around the wire just under her chin.

"No ... not the blood." SNAP! "It's not the blood at all, Reed. I see too much emotion. There's no art here, only savagery."

"Art?"

"Yes, Reed, art. There's a difference. Pathological-crazy-person speaking, that is." That was what we were dealing with, Reed finally admitted, and the business at hand was a repulsive one, one of the worst I had ever seen in my ten years of forensic photography. She had been arched over backwards — snapped in half — her limbs manipulated and twisted, her bones bent into awkward postures, and her skin had been ripped open. Not sliced or cut but ripped, revealing glistening bloody muscles and sinew. What had once been a young woman, endowed with unlimited innocence and charm, lay there, a perverted mass, leaving only a mere suggestion left behind of the beauty she had once been. An ironic statement so it would seem. "I can't believe you got me out of bed for this, Reed. Fuck me."

"Exactly."

"Exactly what?"

"Exactly, fuck me," was his only retort.

Candles of all sizes, shapes, and colors circled the body, as if paying homage to that which was to succumb to ruin, and a rosary lay across her stomach. Alms for a poor soul. The onyx beads gently cascading over what was left of the crest of her abdomen, the image of Christ on the cross lost within her entrails. SNAP!

"I see too much…"

"Too much what, Rowan?"

"Too much anger," I replied without even thinking what I was saying. I wasn't a detective. What was I looking for? Who was I to make assumptions? I'm no one. I just record the scene. That's all I do, so I crouched down and leaned in a little closer. Tried not to inhale.

A spider's web of veins had risen to the surface, imparting to her skin the blue-black tinge of a beating gone cold. A sharp contrast in color to the pools of coagulated blood that had sunk through the fibers of the mattress clear to the floor. I switched my camera to my left hand and then reached forward to lift the veil from her face. When I did, I almost fell off my feet. Insect larvae. Eyes, ears, mouth, like gaping wounds, wriggling and writhing within mounds of shed exoskeletons and excrement. She had been here for a while. The sands of time and decay had already begun to claim her.

Over and over again, the people in the local village would whisper, "She was a lovely girl." Young, beautiful, a charming demeanor. Her hair flaming red, luscious, and vibrant. Her eyes at one time had been a pristine emerald green. Her hips and breasts voluptuous, and her skin, alabaster and dusted with flecks of sunshine. A lovely girl, reduced to horrid bits of nothing. Less than nothing. Worse than nothing. A rotted morsel for the eaters of the dead. A lovely girl … was that all?

Was that all she was to them?

"Did anyone really know her at all, Reed? In the village? Because IT did, the monster who violated her. All that polite euphemistic nonsense about her loveliness. It wasn't her loveliness that had seduced this thing. Even if she were the biggest flirty cock-tease in town, that doesn't warrant this. Such savagery, such a deliberate lack of humanity. Sixty stab wounds by my count, Reed. It's as if it were trying to cut the kindness and purity from her womb. It hadn't simply wanted to violate her. It had wanted to destroy her." SNAP!

"What is it, Rowan?"

I thought I had said, "The past—" before Reed extended a hanky filled hand. "You ok, kid? Here … put this over your nose. It'll stop the gagging. That's it. Sorry about the aftershave. Wife doesn't like the stink of death on me. Now what were you saying about the past?"

"It's never really the past, is it, Reed? Through the lens, I mean. She'll never rest, and we'll never be rid of this memory."

"No, Rowan. It isn't, and we won't, and it's a damn shame we've got nothing but this."

"This is enough."

I spent another hour or so committing the gruesome scene to film before the nausea overtook me and I had to venture into that tiny room with its torturous dripping tap. I even had a plastic bag so I could vomit and not contaminate the scene. A soothing fucking notion, Reed would say. Vomiting is a natural biological response to offensive stimuli. It is not a state of mind nor is it always indicative of systemic illness, which in Reed-speak meant it was one less thing to worry about or be ashamed of.

I didn't have to worry about it though, the moment I stumbled into the tiny closet of a washroom, the smell of rot smacked into me immediately, even before I could slip in the mung covering the floor. The stench was so powerful I could taste it. So overwhelming it was that my mind, in a state of sensory confusion, misplaced the feeling of nausea that had gripped me only moments before. My tongue swelled, and my eyes burned as acid tears seared their sockets. The air was so dense and oppressive that you could scrape it from the walls. My visit to this room would be a brief one, that, or Inspector Reed would be scraping my body from the floor.

I spit several stringy gobs of stomach acid and bile into the bag and then looked to the mirror above what was left of a washbasin, which jutted precariously out from the wall, balanced weightlessly in mid-air by the rusted iron pipe beneath it. Beaten mercilessly by time, slick and stained with old blood and numerous unidentifiable oily secretions, the tap dripped, rhythmically, pounding out a totemic song of anguish and despair.

I looked up. Stared at my reflection in the mirror's fractured glass. It too was fading, fading into bleak undiscovered depths. "Death warmed over." That's what Reed always said I looked like just after a shoot. My skin, a lovely greenish patina, withered over my bones, and there was a monstrous hostility to my eyes.

Not my eyes.

They were his eyes I was looking into in that mirror. Wild and luminous. He had washed his hands in this very sink, washed them delicately, not to make them clean but to rejuvenate the dried blood on them in order to paint his face like a demon cast out from the depths of hell.

He dreamt he was a demon…

He dreamt it while awake.

I looked into those eyes again, but he just sneered at the thinly veiled image of himself, of me. He sneered with dry, bloody lips drawn back over yellowed and rotted teeth. Teeth worn down by the bones of his victims, which he gnawed down to the marrow, and through the raggedy sweat-soaked tendrils of greasy hair that fell over his forehead, he picked at the flesh of his face, dismantling bit by bit the distance between us.

I could see him as clearly as if he were inside of me, looking out at me through my own eyes, and I through his. I felt the rage, the satisfaction, the hunger. I felt it as if it were my own, and that was worse.

Worse than being gnawed on in the darkness.

YOU HAD BORNE THE WEIGHT OF IT
With arrogant pride,
And it had dragged you down.

2

Shake Hands *with the Devil*

After stepping back outside, I sucked the fresh air into my lungs as fast as was possible. So fast that it made me lightheaded. My only thought was to find myself as far away from this dreadful place as I could imagine. How fortunate for me that my imagination had quite a far reach.

The path in the direction of away was neglected and weedy, and it eventually, along with my thoughts, lost itself into an abandoned field. As I made my way further and further from the cottage, the sun, high in the sky now, seemed to be reaching out for me. It hit my shoulders with a gentle warmth, expanding the distance between my soul and the horror it had just been forced to witness. The comfort was a welcome relief. The ochre-drenched blossoms of the leopards-bane, the drooping rain-laden petals of the sky-blue chicory flowers, even the despicable weeds — from the tenacious cockleburs to the gnarled, thorny raspberry brambles — all reached out to me, all desired to embrace me, to offer me some respite in their beauty.

As I walked, I spied dainty pale blue flax vying for notice over the alkanet's lavender splendor as it pushed its way upwards through spires of switch grass, and I smiled what felt like a very small and humble smile. How I longed to hold on to this image of perfection and serenity. Nature's innate peace and tranquility, always offering that to us she is like a fleeting glimpse of hope, clinging to the wildflowers like dew.

The first blush of spring is so fleeting.

So easily tainted.

A wisp of wind swept through the trees lining the path. The winter had been too cold this past year. Many couldn't recover from it, and some … some barely noticed it at all, the cold sting of the first frost now all but forgotten. Swarms of bees hummed as they diligently marauded the wild hyssop, while butterflies teetered through the air on drunken wings. The soft, velvety grass muffled the sound of my footsteps, just as it must have muffled the echo of her screams.

Bloodcurdling screams in the night.

I could hear them. In my mind, and a shiver pricked over my flesh. I felt cold again, but I pressed onward, hard, looking only forward, never back. I stopped only for a brief moment to light a cigarette. Not because I actually needed to smoke but in a rather simplistic attempt to burn the rancid taste of that bathroom from my mouth. I was glad that I had, and as I rolled the mentholated smoke slowly over my tongue, my nerves, much affected by the gruesome scene in the cottage, were instantly relieved. *Not too much longer of a walk back to my car now. Just a few more steps away.* Just beyond that huge bale of hay, my junker was there waiting for me. There is nothing like the oily, rusted out stink of an old motorcar. Time beaten, sweaty leather. Stale cigarette butts crowding the ashtray. Pollen dust tinting the windows, inside and out. It's a comforting filth, and it was my filth, so I was grateful for it instead of being mindful of it. It also meant I could finally put this place and its evil stench behind me.

Door wide open so that the breeze might refresh me, I sank back into the driver's seat while I gathered up the rolls of film and placed them into the labeled evidence bag. My next stop would be the station house in order to release the film to the lab and transfer the chain of custody. I tossed the bag on the passenger seat, pulled the door closed, and started the motor, which only chugged and clunked a little in complaint, nothing a quick pedal to the floorboards couldn't cure.

Despite the choking blue-grey smog now dissipating around my car, it really was a lovely day, so perfect in every way that my retreat need not be too hasty, and so I reached up and adjusted the rear-view mirror. I wanted to look at my face, maybe fuss with my hair a little in hopes of restoring to my appearance some semblance of respectability and professionalism, but my own weary, troubled eyes were not the ones casting their reflection back at me. *I am not alone.*

As I stared into that mirror, I felt my fingers tighten around the steering wheel. So tight with both hands that the blood had slipped away from my knuckles. I wanted to bear down on the accelerator, but my mind had locked up in a confusion of questions and absurd crime drama scenarios. *How did he get in the backseat of my car?* Had I left it unlocked? *I am so forgetful.* I invited him in. *Held the door open for him.* If I could just move, I thought, or run. If I could just blink. Maybe that might make him go away, but I couldn't seem to tear my eyes away from his. Eyes that possessed the fury of a monster not a man. Bloated with blood, the veins, thick and clotted, obliterated the whites of those eyes, and for the life of me, I could not stop myself falling into their hideous and hypnotic depths as he slowly leaned forward to reach and wrap his forearm across my chest, pinning me to the seat as he clenched my shoulder with his right hand and then pressed his face against mine. My skin went cold and clammy, and a flood of warm saliva filled my mouth as his heated breath sprayed my neck with filth and foulness.

Fighting seemed impossible. Reason, logic, seemed impossible. I struggled little and whimpered less as he pressed his face in harder, the razor sharp stubble on his chin digging into my cheek, but a glint of sunlight in the rear-view mirror caught my eye and distracted me from my predicament for a second. A second to realize that glint had reflected off the hunting knife he held in his hand. He noticed that my eyes had wandered from his, that the blade now had my undivided attention, so he turned it this way and that, allowing the now menacing sun to cast it aglow for my appreciation. As demented and terrifying as the thought was, it occurred to me that I was probably the only one who could appreciate it, and he smiled a callous and satisfied smile.

Yes, he seemed satisfied. Its beauty and dark intent revealed to me, he raised the knife to his eye, and, with slow precision, inserted the tip into his left eyeball. A yellow puss oozed from the gouged opening. Sticky and gelatinous, it slipped down along the ridge of his cheekbone, which jutted out sharply from the hollow flesh of his face.

I began to struggle, or at least I thought I did. Everything felt numb, like my body had no bones. I was no match for him. His arm held me in place as tightly as if I were strapped to the seat with a mile of gaffer tape, a mouthful of rotted teeth pressed to my ear — smiling — as he dug the knife in a little deeper.

Spittle on my neck.

He was laughing now…

No sound.

His mouth gaped widely, splitting his face in two, but there was no sound at all. Even the desperate pounding of my own heart fell muted as if plunged into an abyss.

I just have to step on the accelerator.

But my foot wouldn't obey my command.

Why wouldn't my foot obey my command?

It felt like a club of flesh. *My foot had been amputated.* That must be it, and I was left only with a weighted club, but it had been fashioned too heavy, and so I couldn't lift it, not with all of my strength. *I just can't lift it.*

Why wasn't I strong enough to lift it?

Oh God!

With a sharp flick of his wrist, he cut the eyeball completely out of its socket and flung it at the windscreen. It hit with a resounding thud as threads of mucus sprayed outwards in a web across the glass. I felt it stipple the skin of my face, and I screamed — louder now — I screamed again. Then he vanished, leaving only the haunting figure of a raven, stomping on the hood of my car.

I might not have been able to pry my hands from the steering wheel at that moment, but I had certainly found my foot again. I hit the accelerator, and after mustering the last bit of strength left in my voice, I shouted, "Fuck you, you ghastly beast..." as the raven hit the windscreen full on and tumbled over the roof, at which point I bid it a fond farewell. Good riddance, I thought with much relief. "...and fuck the god-forsaken shadow you rode in on as well," I said as loud as I could manage through the churning dust and road rubble left behind in my wake.

YOU HAD PRETENDED TO UNDERSTAND IT,
And it, sharp against your mind,
Had pretended to understand you.

3

Apathy

I t took a while before I realized that I was moving faster than the speed limit permitted, but every muscle in my body felt as taut as starched rope, making conscious control of my reflexes impossible. I had tunnel vision on top of that.

The scenery blurred, rushing past me almost unnoticed. I was lost. Seeing but not really seeing. It would be a lingering mind-numbing trip back to the station, and for obvious reasons, I had no thoughts about anything other than the unsteady rhythm of my heartbeat and the wicked shimmer of the madman's knife caught in the back of my eye.

From dirt road to paved, civilization crawled out

from the wilderness, casting its pestilent shadow over the windswept grassy fields and hedgerows. Heavily trafficked intersections, herds of affected people, and the shimmering stark facades of modern office buildings — the overflowing cesspit of humanity — would eventually overtake and obliterate the small towns with their pubs and quaint local shops.

By the time I reached the city, I had already developed an extreme case of claustrophobia and a rather nasty bit of halitosis from the bad taste the city always leaves in my mouth. I parked the car, fed the meter glittering sustenance, hunched my shoulders up over my head, and made with a non-invasive approach towards the crowded intersection.

No one even looked at me.

By the time I slunk through the doors of the station house, the flood of emotion and nausea had released its hold on me, replaced with a soothing sense of apathy. My non-emotion of choice.

The large crowded building was a terminal assault on the senses. It roared with banal chitchat, heated conversations, and all manner of goings on, not to mention the overpowering and constant clicking and stomping of footsteps, echoing back on themselves as they reverberated up and down staircases and along high, cathedral-ceilinged corridors.

Inordinately loud voices battled against each other for higher and higher position amidst the din. Pencils, taking no refusal, bore down, pushing their lead willfully against forms of duplicate and triplicate copies. Fingers smashed diligently against keyboards, and endless stacks of papers whispered and sighed as they were savagely pillaged while overhead fans, motors groaning with dutiful disdain, moved molecules of sweat and disgust throughout the stagnant air.

My destination: the second floor.

Uniformed people, starched and pressed like proper planks of wood, stood about, patiently awaiting the lift while engrossed in idle chit-chat. The status of the weather. The latest football scores. Numbing their minds by way of avoidance to drown out what was actually going on in their heads.

I hate lifts. Absolutely hate the damn things. Nothing but steel clad skips, flinging you to and fro throughout time and space with nothing to hold on to but the hope that it won't send you careening to your demise amidst a heap of tangled wreckage. Painful death aside, I wasn't very fond of idle chatter either, so I took the stairs.

Shifts were changing as I made my way down the infinitely stretching corridor to the evidence room. There was a lot of scribbling. Hurried and illegible signatures. A lot of duty roster scanning, accompanied by groaning, pointing, and sighing at the grisly inevitabilities of the day ahead. No one really noticed me, except for the occasional offhanded glance at the credentials hanging around my neck. I am technically a civilian after all, and in the civilian world, going unnoticed is a good thing. Blending into the banality is sometimes the best and only defense against the static.

At long last, I reached the glass enclosed evidence desk. The fishbowl, as I like to call it, except today the only fish in the bowl was not the sort that put you in awe. The woman behind the counter lifted her head and glared at me with pinched face and pursed lips. "Picking up or dropping off?" she said, her voice harsh. An old woman's regret ground over sandpaper, and it seeped through the holes in the glass in plume of sewer stench. I wondered what would happen if I covered the holes? My hand began reaching for the glass with a will and determination of its own. "Dropping off," I answered, smiling broadly at the thought of her impending suffocation. Would she flap about on the laminate floor? If she did, at least the irony would amuse me.

She screwed up her eyes at me before her mouth popped open to inquire, "What department?" in a tone so blatantly accusing, as if I were attempting to assess her psychic abilities, which I wasn't. She had barely an ability, even for common speech, or she would have phrased her questions in a more polite open-ended manner. I was mocking her. So what. If she weren't such a rat's nest of a human being, people might think better of her and treat her with a little more respect. However, considering the morning I had endured, it was not the sort of day for tutelage in fine manners.

"Who shoved the stick up your ass?" was the only question I could think of that amounted to anything, and I really don't know why I had bothered asking. It didn't really matter to me who shoved it there or what sort of stick it was, actually. We all have our crosses to bear, I guess. I simply didn't need to be catching splinters from it. "The photo-lab for fuck' sake, I am dropping off film for the photo-lab."

I heard the lock buzz on the door.

"Come round then," she instructed, but now there was less sourness to her tone.

I mentioned something earlier about expectations, so what could I hope to expect. She was riddled with road burn. Considering her toxic personality, I would have liked to strap her to the bumper of my car by her ankles and drag her through some gravel myself. As I contemplated that idea, Cameron, one of the photo-lab technicians, came barreling up to the counter. The rubber soles of his shoes sent a piercing squeal into the air as he demanded his feet come to a full stop directly beside me. The rat's nest just glowered at us and shoved a few forms in my general direction. Then she went back to clicking her talons on the computer keyboard. If a smile could be sarcastic, well, I gave her that one, along with a sigh made of lead. She turned and threw me a piercing look, as if I had ruined the moment, let alone her whole damn day. So let's just consider that I had ruined it, why not make the most of it and dig in a bit more? I do have principles.

"A writing implement perchance, Doris, or do you want me to sign the forms in spit?"

She slammed a pen down onto the counter and then stuck an accusatory stare to me as if I were some sort of gangster. Maybe I should scratch my ass with the pen. Or pick my nose with it. Cameron chuckled as if he had heard my thoughts. He hadn't. He had his own amusement in mind.

"Hey Rowan, what's on the meat menu for today?"

You wouldn't think that he would be so nasty and spry with all the curly auburn hair and freckles, but that smile he had always gave him away. I kept my eyes focused on Doris as I teasingly twirled the pen about in my fingers.

"Oh, she's gorgeous, Cam. I think you'll like her."

"Ah," he exclaimed with raised arm and a romantic lilt, "but will I fall madly in love?"

His twisted smile could not be helped, and neither could mine. "You need a fucking psychiatrist, you know that, Cameron."

"So everyone tells me." He scribbled his signature on the forms, grabbed the bag of film, and then set himself into a high-speed freestyle dash back down the hallway, mumbling incoherent words into his own vortex as he went. All I managed to work out through the torrent was, "Lunch. You and me, Rowan. Lunch."

Judging by the look on her face, I was sure that Doris would have liked to eat the both of us. *Fucking bitch cannibal.*

Speaking of therapy … and lunch, I had one more stop to make at the station house. As much as I needed the diversion, lunch with Cameron would not be an option.

YOU WANTED TO POSSESS IT.
But it had used you,
And you had let it.

4

Therapeutic *Malaise*

J on Killkhenny, Ph.D. Part-time police department psychiatrist, full-time head-shrink extraordinaire. The low rent office of. Killy, as I so fondly call him. My lover of a sorts and a righteous pain in the ass. I should have had a cigarette beforehand. *Still had time.* So what if I was a wee bit late? Missed the appointment altogether. I knocked once and then reluctantly opened the door. *Fuck.* I should have had that cigarette, but it was too late now. There he was the cheeky bastard, sitting on the corner of his antique mahogany desk, one leg up, tap, tap, tapping the face of his watch with a marauding and insolent glint in his eyes. You couldn't help but get caught in them. Coal-black and vacuous eyes he had, mirroring the echo of a bottomless pit. The loose wisps of black hair falling deliberately over them didn't soften that stare, either. He invoked command in every casual gesture. My Killy, always mildly annoyed yet above all that mattered to him. Stylish. Graceful. Fearsome in his detachment. He had a potent and mysterious seductiveness that could lull you into a dangerous and obsessive state of anticipation. One that made me think that I really should have had that cigarette.

"Lock the door," he insisted with brute dryness, so I pushed the door closed behind me and turned the lock. The chill of the steel clung to the tips of my fingers, and the catch of the bolt resonated in my ears like a failed acquittal, bringing with it a hot sweaty sense of exhilaration mixed with dread. I felt a very bad decision coming on, and I knew he could smell it. My hand hadn't even left off the doorknob before he was all over me, pressing the full weight of his body against mine, grinding the stink of his cheap cologne into my clothes, and as usual, the battle of the sexes ensued with a mad struggle. Clothes, desperately clawed from flailing limbs, falling limply to the floor. Hips and knees pushing against each other. There was nothing of love in the misery of it, nothing but flesh beset with tooth and nail, then a slightly off kilter pirouette wronged and then righted by the forces of gravity, ending in a series of brutal thrusts, disguising words gaping mouths slick with saliva and sweat dared not speak to one another. The last assault of passion waxed in a crest of delirium then waned in a whimper, a cry of agony, and then silence.

We disentangled from one another, and he backed away from me as if he were allowing me to regain my dignity. Well, it was either that or he was feeling some hint of disgust for indulging in such animalistic behavior. Scrabbling at me like some rabid dog want for a bone with meat on it. *Who was the psycho now, Doctor?* His eyes distant, elsewhere. He was probably mulling over what Freud would have had to say about the sorry sordid affair, so I slid off the desk, turned my bare ass towards him, and then I moved in the direction of the sofa.

"Put your knickers on, Rowan, you'll ruin the suede," he said in a low heaven-forbid-that-I-soil-the-luxurious-nutmeg-colored-suede-of-his-designer-sofa tone of voice. He retrieved a spray can of furniture polish from his desk drawer and began a mad attempt to buff away the residue of our encounter. I just glared at him, sat down, and ground my dripping wet cunt into the upholstery.

"Nice, Rowan, very nice." He maintained his death-dry business tone and composure as he buffed away like a madman. "So, do you want to talk about what you saw today?"

He had to be kidding, right? I did not want to talk about what I had seen, this day, that day, or any other day. I never wanted to do that, and he knew it. The only reason I was there, in the building at all, was to drop off the film. I really don't know why I had even bothered stopping in to see him. *Standing appointment. What a joke.* I should have questioned his professionalism in that moment. Shirt open. Trousers undone. Hair a disheveled mess. I was sure there was an ethics issue smeared all over that desktop somewhere. Although, he did not seem to share my viewpoint on the matter. He zipped up his trousers and then looked at me with prying expectant eyes as he began buttoning his shirt, so what was I going to say? "I saw a fucking doorstop today, same as every other day, Killy. You know that."

He couldn't suppress the look of disgust that overspread his face. He tossed the furniture polish back into the drawer and kicked the drawer closed before stepping boldly into his high and mighty dissertation, "Why do you torture yourself with this job? Mangled bodies. It's all just mangled bodies, and don't go on about Karma and cosmic duty because of Rhys. Rhys is dead, Rowan. You were children. It was an accident, and you didn't have a relationship with him. It never got started. Rowan, are you listening to me? Let's be serious here. You have to stop dwelling in this creep show of a world that you're living in. It's not healthy ... and frankly, it's downright gruesome. You need to stop taking pictures of death and actually start living a life." He placed his hands on his hips as he awaited my reply. I wasn't sure I had one, flippant or otherwise, not to mention whether or not he even deserved one.

Children? Were we just children, or did we know something, feel something beyond ourselves that day on the bridge? That cold stone bridge, spanning the chasm of ... what? A life that was to be and a life that could never be. Or could it have been? I didn't have the answer now any more than I had it then. It was a pointless answer I was seeking, anyway. A construct, a fabrication. A lie. Or was it? *'I want to marry you, Rowan, when we get older, when we can ... I want to ... do you want to?'* I remember those words, broken with emotion as they fell from his lips that day. *Just children.* What do children know of life, love, and desperation? Nothing. She couldn't even remember now if she had answered. It might have been only a breath, no more than a logical reflex. *"No."* Did she say it? She couldn't be sure. She could never be sure. Of course she hadn't said it, and even if she had, the evil of the world had stifled all sound that day. No leaves rustling in the trees, no bird's melancholy phrases echoing in the breeze. No breeze. Even the water of the river below had stilled itself … as had the beating of her heart.

"Rowan!"

The depth and breadth of Killy's voice put my mind on pause. *We were having a conversation?* Of course, and if I remembered correctly, it was a heated conversation, so I leapt on his words rather carelessly, "Shit Killy, did you just tell me what I need? Don't tell me what I need. I don't need action plans. I don't need feedback. I don't need to talk through anything, and I certainly don't need self-actualization. I know what I need. I just need to get shagged every once in a while, and you service that need quite satisfactorily."

He drew himself up out of his chair, his face colored with blotches of red. He rarely showed any emotion beyond condescension, so it was nice to see a flicker of life occasionally. He placed his hands on the desk, palms down, and leaned over, leering at me with inhuman malice. His threatening, hardened posture slapped me across the face even more violently than his words. "I will allow that this once, but only this once because of the state you're in, Rowan, so don't do that again. Don't reduce me like that. I am not at your service."

"I'm sorry," I said, but it was a lie. Even though his words seemed to beg for an apology, that wasn't really what he wanted. He didn't want a request for forgiveness; he wanted an admission of guilt. That wasn't something I could give, not to him. I wasn't sorry. I hated it when he accused me of being affected, but if it eased the tension even a bit then it wasn't such an awful thing — to lie.

His shoulders relaxed, and then he sat back down in his chair. "No need to apologize. We should get away for a while, to the country house. You can take a break and take pictures of the scenery, read some poetry or something."

I just stared at the floor and fumbled for my lighter.

"Can't smoke in here; you know that, Rowan. Policy, Rowan. Damn it, policy!"

I felt hot again. It wasn't the tone of his voice that irritated me so, it was the lack of it, and so any shred of decorum I might have held onto slipped by the wayside. I stumbled, flailing fists first into a fit of rage. "Killy, Doctor, you just slammed your cock into me for a half an hour, you don't seriously think you're in a position to make demands let alone invoke policy. Piss on policy. Open a bloody window if you're going to be a twat about it."

I finished my cigarette lost amidst the quagmire of his cold, smug gaze. He said not a word to me, so I stood up, flicked my cigarette butt out through the window, picked my trousers up from the floor, and put them on. In one last move of defiance, I flung my knickers at him, and then I turned and made my way towards the door, where I struggled feverishly in a futile attempt at escape.

The door obviously aimed to deny me my need for a hasty and dignified retreat. "It's locked, Rowan." He leaned back in his chair and grinned. This I knew, without even needing to turn around.

"You're knee deep in your own smug, you know that, Killy. You are such a belligerent fucker, and I hope that crap attitude of yours sucks you down."

I unlatched the bolt and the door swung inward with a gust of fresh un-sexually charged air. I wanted out, but for some unknown reason, my foot faltered at the threshold. He would have only a moment to make his last plea.

"Rowan." His placating tone hit me sharp in the spine.

"What? What on earth do you want from me, Killy?"

"Supper … later?"

I knew he was grinning from ear to ear now, arrogant full of himself pain-in-the-hole, and he knew I wouldn't turn around to give him the satisfaction of witnessing it.

"Yeah, alright," I said, accepting the invitation with the appropriate amount of contrived shame, and without looking back, I walked out of his office, jerking the door closed with such force that his distinguished name plaque went swinging precariously by the last tiny nail that held it in place.

YOU WITHHELD SECRETS,
Hoping it would starve to death.

5

A Moment *in the Shadows*

I loaded another roll of film into my camera and then
drove down the tree-lined street to the local park.
You know the sort of place. All wrought-iron gates
and preserved open space. An urban oasis, maintained by
the trust fund managers of the egregiously wealthy and
the eternally deceased. A place whereby one can get back
to nature. Well, it's not really nature. It's more of a mangy
menagerie of sickly half-feathered birds, lice-laden
ground squirrels, and stray cats, down on their haunches,
stalking their prey as if caught in a surreal dream of the
African Savannah. If that's what you call nature, then I
suppose it is.

Sharing the last scraps of stale bread with the equally

diseased waterfowl, old vagrants occupied every single bench in the place, that stale bread being the only food they've been able to get their grubby mitts on for weeks, and yet, they choose to share it unselfishly with any creature that happens to stumble by. A wish for wings, I suppose. Feeding the birds might actually help them to fly. Fly far away from the misery of their own lives, fly far away from themselves, if only in their dreams.

The remainder of the people circulating throughout the park and all about the streets appeared nothing more than half-alive to me. The walking dead. Hurtling their vacant faces and their equally vacant minds through the day too quickly to take even the slightest notice of the miraculous beauty before them. Or even notice the trash at their feet, for that matter, as gratuities were being exchanged, trinkets wrapped and bagged for transport. Fucking tourists. Belching and passing wind on street corners and in front of shop windows. Whining and blathering incomprehensibly ridiculous drivel. Those sausages were so very delicious, wouldn't you say? Isn't the architecture simply wonderful? Yes, it's absolutely astounding. Let's cross the street to that lovely park and watch the penniless street-people feed the winged rats. Maybe we'll see a poor child. Will he look like Oliver Twist? How quaint.

In complete and utter disgust, I made my way to an undisturbed area of the park. A small grotto plunged deeply into the shade by the stretching branches of the elm trees. There was a stone bench tucked into the tall grass and weeds, which overlooked a fetid pond, its still surface covered in a thick film of algae. Barely a creature could survive the abysmal depths of this tiny swamp.

Choked of oxygen, the few fish residing in the murk gasped at the surface in a fury of open mouths and tail fins. This was my favorite place to take ease for some reason. A neglected and weedy patch of the park, too dismal and macabre for most people to find any solace. As I approached the bench, I could see a figure sitting alone there. Apparently, I had stumbled upon another unfortunate parody, lost in the catacombs of his own mind.

He paid me no notice as I sat down beside him, and I sat there for a while, watching the drowning fish until I became bored chucking crumbs at them, so offhandedly, while stretching my arms, I took a look at the man next to me. It was just a quick glance, but almost immediately, I felt something stir within me. It wasn't really a feeling or a conscious thought, just a muddled sense of something, and I felt sad. I hadn't felt sad about anything in a long time, so I looked at him more thoughtfully, as he didn't seem to mind the intrusion. He was old. Faded and flaking. Like one of those paintings in a museum. He was thin, stoop-shouldered, a cripple of a man, dressed in a shabby tweed suit, which was fraught with moth damage and much too thin for the early spring weather. An equally frayed cap sat precariously atop his head, holding down the almost comically thin strands of white hair that spilled out from underneath it and whipped wildly at his face in the wind. His wife used to cut his hair away from his face, but now she didn't. I don't know how I knew that, but I just did, and I really wanted to touch that face. There was something odd about it. I mean, every face is peculiar to a degree, except a dead face. A dead face is just that. Frozen in resignation. Living faces are downright bursting with emotion. They are perfectly readable even at a distance, but with this old man, every line and indentation — lines that should have indicated age and wisdom — seemed dull and expressionless. Either from a life of obsessive contemplation — or resigned futility — his deeply creased forehead receded so greatly it seemed more like a time-ravaged granite sculpture than a human face. His rough and severely pitted cheeks appeared more pronounced in the waning light, more burdened with regret than any face I'd seen before. A regret that couldn't be forgiven or forgotten. One that time couldn't erode with idealized memories. To add further to his state of disarray, he looked as if a maniac had given him a Sunday shave with various assorted rusty garden tools.

Even so, I couldn't look away, and in a moment, I found myself looking directly into his eyes and he into mine. Watery, jaundiced green eyes that had lost the will to blink let alone see the world for what it was. He was hideously beautiful. He was death's sublime poetry, a verse no one dares whisper until it's much too late to appreciate. I looked towards the ground in a show of sympathy, and that's when I noticed his hands. I couldn't help myself and reached out for them. They reached back as he slid closer to me and I to him until we were tucked into each other. My own hands looked frail and small next to his, which were gnarled like claws, heavily veined, thin skinned, and covered in open sores and wounds. They were hands that had worked once, hands that had loved and sacrificed once. Hands now torn to shreds by a thousand hungry beaks and talons. The birds swarmed and groveled at his feet, kicking the dust up and about his shoes, which pointed inward, like the feet of a shy abandoned child.

I felt a sense of kinship with him in some inexpressible way. His shabby clothes mirrored the state of my soul in every frayed seam. Maybe it was the bitter knowledge that neither one of us had a choice but to be what we were. We both shared the same desires. To exist like the murky pond. To be satisfied with stale, filthy breadcrumbs. To have no more. To want no more. I could see behind his eyes. Could see the desire to be as dead on the outside as he felt on the inside. The desire not to be.

"It was you," he said, "escaped from the hospital, wounded, leash still around your neck. You were but a girl then, muslin lightly rubbing against your knees, and you dreamt of Dostoyevsky while walking barefoot in the wilderness that sultry summer night. I knew you then, unlike I know you now."

I didn't know him, and I didn't know what he meant by that, but I felt ashamed anyway. I'd never told anyone about my stay in the ward, and I didn't want to think of it now, but he just stared at me, waiting. If it weren't for the light temperate breeze moving over us, I wouldn't have been able to tear my eyes away from his pathetic face and the smile on it that had lingered a little too long. It was as if he knew a secret so old and so desperate it could change the world. My world. The thought of it troubled me, but there was that breeze, gently running its fingers through and along the cracks of time and space, and it carried his decrepit odor directly to my nose, thankfully drowning out the stench of the pond. He smelled of stale tobacco and rancid milk. I had smelled worse that day, and at least his perfume had the sweet smell of life, as spare as it was. "Ten for a photo," I offered, to which he turned and offered me another toothless smile in return for my generosity. So it was agreed. I lifted my camera.

SNAP!

"I killed my wife, you know," he said without pause or inflection, and my response to his confession leapt off my lips without so much as a thought, "I know," I replied, "and it doesn't really matter, in the twilight."

In my younger days, I had often romanticized that word: twilight. I feared the twilight now. That time in between the dark and the light, where everything exists in whispers and frightened prayer. It was that time now, and the old man stood just beyond the edge of my bed, half in and half out of the darkness, gripping the footboard with those huge bleeding hands. I could hear him, talking to the shadows in a hauntingly hollow voice. "My name is Gaunt," came his voice on a whisper in a shock of cold air to my left ear. "Sir Gaunt to you, if you've got a terminal illness to sell. I'm always looking to barter for a bag of bones, if you got one. Do you got one, Rowan? I command the legions, you see, and for a wee small fee, they obey … only me." He reached down and waved his hand over the blanket, and it was then that I felt them. Hordes of tiny barbed feet swarming over my sweat-soaked body, digging, gouging into my flesh. I felt them, scrapping and gnawing at my shins and my ankles, and when I kicked the covers from my legs, there were leaches slithering all over my thighs through a mixture of blood, saliva, and primordial ooze. My flesh had no substance. It was dissolving before my eyes into a pulpy, glutinous mass of rotted meat, blistering and bulging with flies, maggots, and other foul, demonic vermin. The bed was infested with them. The eaters of the dead. They had come for me, come to breed under my skin, turn my brain to blood pudding, and suck out my eye sockets so that I might only see the blackness of the world. "It's not real," I whispered to myself, but my mind strained against my own words, and so I clenched my eyes shut as tightly as I could.

It's not real...

I knew it wasn't. Killy was breathing next to me, contemptuously to the rhythm of his own chaotic dreams. I could smell him. The heat of him had soaked the bed sheets through with the sour stench of curdled sex. Semen. Pheromones. Sweat. He mumbled a few incoherent words and then flung his arm across my chest. An embrace that made me feel empty. Stripped of my dignity yet again by this witchdoctor whom I called my lover.

Yes ... I would surely be eaten alive.

The crawling shadow of darkness dominated everything, had dominated everything in my life for as long as I could remember. Heavy and unyielding it moved over the walls, the floor, and the ceiling. I could feel it moving over me, into me. Could taste it in my mouth. Gamey. Week old rot. They would feast upon me, and it would be a magnificent feast. So there I lay, in that empty space, hands over my ears, waiting ... waiting for my body to fall apart. It felt like I was falling, but the descent was so slow and measured that the distance between my memories and every past moment of time in my life seemed imperceptible, as if those moments didn't seem to matter, didn't seem to exist. It was that weightless feeling, of flying, of dying ... of being born anew.

In the past few months, my dreams have taken on the remnants of a dementia worse than madness. Scattered illusions and delusions. Nothing more than windblown filaments. An imaginary web of twisted, fragmented, and disordered thoughts and memories. I knew all this. The logic was not lost on me, but logic doesn't change anything.

So there I lay, a fool, cowering in my bed, the dread swirling around me like a black tempest. When sleep came, finally plunging me into the void, I fell aimlessly into it, drenched in the cold sweat of my own misshapen reality, and for all its horror, it didn't matter.

IT HAD BETRAYED YOU,
And you despised it.

6

Witness

May 27, 1998

J ust a girl on a bridge, petticoat billowing in the wind at her knees. He loves me ... He loves me not, she thought on a petal, softly, gently, as it winged its way down through sunbeams, laughter, and the swift buzzing of dragonfly wings to settle on the water below. She thought them fairies, the dragonflies, borne of childhood wishes, their wings glittering over the water like a thousand stained-glass rainbows. Buzzing and buzzing...

But it was the phone, constantly buzzing. A digital intrusion. A rude and abrupt end to my dreams. Nightmares actually, and I had yet to find reason enough to ignore them and the damn phone.

Overcast with shadows, the stark stillness of the room thrust an abrupt realization upon me in that moment. I couldn't recall the last time I had a decent night's sleep, let alone sweet or pleasant dreams, but the buzzing continued unabated despite this salient tidbit and my half-hearted fumbling in the almost-dark. Obviously, it wasn't going to stop, so I hit the green button and placed it to my ear. "Rowan," I said hoarsely, but the salutation at the other end of the line was just mumbling. Nothing but angry distorted mumblings assaulting my ear.

I let the phone drop into the twisted, sweat-soaked sheets, and then I rolled over and stared at the ceiling as the early morning sun worked its way through the curtains and flicked across the ceiling, directly aiming to gouge the sleep from my eyes. I had always meant to toss those curtains into the rubbish bin, disgraced rags that they had become, but I could never seem to force myself to part with them. Moth-eaten death shrouds, stiff and outworn. Covered in cobwebs, they lent a grim ambiance to the room. I suppose, all things considered, I wouldn't have liked them any other way. However, crack-house fashion statement that they were, they weren't enough to hold my attention, and my eyes wandered back to the ceiling, but even the minimalist dignity of its surface offered me little respite. So it would be it seemed, another day filled with more fodder for my nightmares. At least Killy had had the decency to slink off in the night like the dog he was.

I threw off the sheets, sat up, and cast my legs over the edge of the bed with a sigh of defeat. Yes. The day had defeated me again, before it had even begun. All of the days before and behind me blend into one another.

Today, tomorrow, next week, or last Tuesday. Their temporal subtleties are indistinguishable to me now. There is no time, no spatial relation for me anymore. My existence is a tenseless blur. Sometimes it feels like an out of body experience. I move in an out of my own history, as if my history could be my future. A vague and distant future without cause or conclusion.

I didn't used to be like this, though. My life wasn't always a stagnant mire. I always had a purpose. Had always had an unwavering clarity of my own, but of late, everything has taken on sort of a muddy hue. The edges burnt and crumbling. The center, too precarious. There is a savage oozing void between my flesh and bone, a void where all of my substance should be, but now there is nothing. The me underneath my skin doesn't feel like me anymore, doesn't even feel human.

I hauled my body from the comfort of my bed and stumbled to the nearby bathroom, my bones cracking the silence of the damp air, my feet leaving vacant impressions on the moist floorboards. Shit, shower, and shave. Isn't that the morning cliché? Why bother, though? Since I would only return home later, vomit, and have to take another shower anyway in a futile attempt to wash the filth and evil from my body, mind, and soul. Nevertheless, the warm water drew the chill out of my bones, so I gave in to its comforts, hoping to let go of the unease settling in my veins for just a moment. The water cascading over me sent the nightmares — my lot as I called them — swirling down the drain, down that dark little rabbit hole from whence they came. A swell of relief washed over me, but the feeling didn't last long though, about as long as the hot water, so I stepped out, toweled off, and then sat down to take a piss. I was still dizzy from the night before. Too much wine. Much too much wine. The lining of my stomach felt raw and scraped out.

I took a deep breath to center myself. The air was warm and wet and soap-scented. It hung about the room, enveloping me in a haze of chamomile and mint. How clean it smelled. Hoping it would linger in my nostrils for the remainder of the day, I inhaled a little deeper, but the calm was interrupted by the pain. Excruciating pain, slicing through my chest.

Too many cigarettes, as well.

I forced myself to my feet, wiped the condensation from the mirror, and took a good long look at my reflection. I hated looking at myself, and yet, I seemed to find myself doing it all the time. My hair, soaked with water, hung in innocent ringlets over my shoulders and into my eyes. My eyes, if they were mine, I couldn't recognize them anymore. Once upon a time, they had been brilliant and clear as the sun's rays shimmering through an autumnal wood. Killy had said that to me once, long ago, when he was into romance and dating. He hasn't said anything like it since.

When had my eyes become so black, so empty?

I am sure on some level it was my fault. I had acquired the leering pitch-black stare of a monster the day I became a witness, and that was a choice I had made. "What does it mean to be a witness?" I asked my reflection, but it had no answers. It never has any answers, just the lean scrawny stare of my shadow reflecting back into me, so I can only speak for myself when I say that it takes a disposition forged of iron to witness the atrocities I have seen. Not that I have an ironclad disposition, I have just never been one of those overly concerned people. Detached, desensitized, maybe. Actually, and you can call me cold if you like, I am generally unconcerned with anything that is not directly in my line of vision, or more to the point, anything that is not in my camera's line of vision. Everything off in the periphery is of little to no consequence to me. My daily existence, this thing I call my life, has evolved into some sort of monstrous pop-up picture book. I relate to the world only in pictures now. Stagnant, emotionless pictures.

Comforting and colorless.

Photography is colorless and comforting. It takes time out of the equation of life. A moment is captured in eternity, allowing you to see, hear, and feel it without all of the white noise and static. Without the fear.

How much does the static influence us?

What about all those things we hear, read, and see on the television. A bit of prose. A passing conversation. A random act of violence. How much of that contaminates us? How much of it affects us to such a degree that we internalize it, choke it down, making it utterly impossible to tell apart from what we had always assumed to be our own identity. Our thoughts and our actions no longer our own but that of the static.

The world we live in is nothing but static.

Humanity — tuned in to the terror, the hypocrisy, and the lies — has nothing to believe in anymore. There is no truth anymore. Only static. The realities of this world can be brutal and cruel. What action man takes to sate his desires — ferocious. There is no compassion, no love, and no understanding. There is only need.

A terrible hungry need.

And what of terror? Real terror. That moment when the thin, flickering shadows reach for you from the darkness. Their bony fingers desiring nothing but to tear at your flesh. Their want only to rip any shred of hope from your soul. The gnashing of their teeth a chaotic din pounding in your ears. It's madness.

"How does one know when they are going mad?" I ask yet again, and again, the silence mocks me. No answer from my shadow. Pointless questions don't deserve answers, I suppose. My own will is nothing more than pointless supposition.

Mostly, I live in some vague altered state of existence. Not dead but not alive. Just numb. I rarely feel anything at all, so tragedy thrills me to no end, and the mix of horror and enthrallment is so heady that it produces an almost surreal and unnatural sense of exhilaration for me. I have always tried to hold fast to the belief that this thrill-seeking need I feel is merely due to an occupation devoid of life. That and a reckless assortment of equally twisted, deviant, and morbid preoccupations, but more and more often lately, the electrified high seems to have faded, and I feel like the victim of some creeping doom. Its misery permeates everything. It clings, slippery, to even the very molecules of the air I breathe.

As I made my way to the kitchen for a cup of tea, my mind slammed into the first of the day's uncomfortable realities: I must be off soon, get in my car, and propel myself to some new memory, a memory I don't want and a memory I certainly don't need. I already have more than enough of those sorts of memories. I put the kettle on, sat down, and then lit a cigarette. I must be off soon, off to commit myself to the unspeakable horror waiting for me. Nightmares they are, validated by mechanical means and sharpened to a gruesome clarity by the lens of my camera. I have borne witness to these abominations with my own eyes, even when I was no longer certain that my eyes still belonged to me. I can't even vouch for my own sanity any longer. Has my life become nothing more than sick and perverted torture porn? Have I witnessed anything of real philosophical value? Or is this life nothing but the mere manifestation of my own guilt, my own self-loathing, and my own hatred. Have I ever known love?

Was it ever my own?

Maybe.

Maybe he was real.

Was he?

Was he ever even with me at all?

I wanted him to be. I needed him to be.

In my mind, he was…

I was convinced of that, if nothing else.

There is no time, no space…

He never tied his shoelaces, but this day … this day, just as many before it, I dried my hair and put it up, the long tendrils now a mass of unruly curls atop my head. Better to keep if out of your face, as you just never know what filth might end up slopping on, what parasites and universal debris might end up clinging to it by the end of the day.

No one ever knows what will cling to them by the end of the day or by the end of a lifetime, for that matter. How could a person know?

Knowing is utterly impossible in the static.

SO YOU LEFT IT THERE…
Without reason,
Without words.

7

A Face Alone *in the Darkness*

he body, if you could call it that, was, at first glance, a mere hump of grey matter chained to a tree. Massive rusted iron links bound the charred remains while maggots undulated amongst the small bits of flesh that hung from gallows of bone.

Another bleak day had dawned, and despite the death and the silence, I still tried to find something beautiful in the moment. A beauty that could delineate the edges, beauty I found so little of in this so-called civilized world. So I closed my eyes and took notice of the wind. It was soft and scented by the cool light rain, which had glossed over every surface. I stood very still, inhaled the damp air, let my mind drift away in shimmering peace, and in that lost moment, I felt warmed by the thrust of dawn even though I feared the diminishing grey spaces and the phantoms that lingered there, still whispering to me through the pitch-black silhouettes of the trees.

Maybe it was the trees that troubled me the most. They seemed to come alive in the indistinct, eerie light as they battled each other, twisting grotesquely, reaching through the fog into some supernatural parallel universe, their gnarled roots clinging resolutely to this one. In the air, I could taste the damp soil, rising up all around me. Moist and lush. Knitting emerald filaments of moss endlessly from trunk to trunk, but no matter how majestic everything seemed to the naked eye, dread had embraced this place. Had made it its own.

Dense and dismal, holding the sky in restraint, the fog had taken reign over everything. One step in the wrong direction and I would be lost and begging the trees for mercy, and judging by the way they tore gashes into the earth, ripping the soil into yawning chasms, I was certain that mercy would be a scarce commodity, let alone the answer to my plea.

I turned once, twice, turning back and around again, seeking a better vantage point. The fog swallowed my breath as I turned, and then I heard it ... a treacherous sound. *Just a murmur but insistent.* Was I the only one who heard it? Crunching. The sound of a thousand tiny jaws chewing what was left of ... *of what?* The wind gusted again, and I realized it was only the leaves. Still clinging haplessly to dead branches, they trembled against each other like a cloud of starving locusts, swarming somewhere in the grey gloom. I attempted to back away from that sound, attempted to escape the torturous din it wielded against the silence all around me, but my heel caught the edge of a gnarled root, and I went reeling backwards into the mud. Apparently, the weather and the state of the forest floor were also beyond my field of vision. Again today, I would suffer the demise of yet another pair of decent shoes.

Filthy, wet, covered in mud, I stood up and then walked the scene, my shoes giving rise to unsettling suction sounds as I heaved them up out of the muck at each step. *Quicksand almost.* This wood was a soul-stealing morass, sucking the life out of me through the soles of my feet.

When I reached the body, I noticed that the branches of the old elm tree he was chained to arched downward, cascading around the torso like a ragged bridal veil, stretching its tendrils in a vain attempt to embrace him. Or to release him. Yet now this tree lay barren, a shadow of its former might, windblown and flayed of its own flesh. Vanquished in its futile attempt, now prostrate and silent.

Had it fed upon his blood as it spilled into the earth?

Now, I am no expert on ghoulish things. I only ask these questions because my soul desperately seeks the answers, often for reasons entirely my own, and in that quest, the way I view a crime scene is sometimes mistaken by others as obsessive, almost an addiction in nature, even though the photographs I take, for the most part, were/are artistically and philosophically meaningful. To me. These sickening and horrifying scenes of subjugation are undoubtedly divine portraits of ascension, the most exquisite aesthetic embodiment of

God as an ideal. Death always is, isn't it? The ancient religious painters had thought as much. Their depictions of the great mortal agony were awe-inspiring, and so, as a self-proclaimed artist, I gave the details of every crime scene the same care I would give the corpse of a loved one. One false or inconsiderate move, one clumsy manipulation would totally destroy any evidence of divine purpose. We can only hope that death has purpose, and great care and devotion must be taken with it.

My devotion is limitless.

I turned full circle taking in the scents, the sounds, and the magnitude of it all, but my body came full stop when I noticed something glistening in the distance. It was a face. A face alone in the darkness. Looking at me. Smiling at me. GRIMACING AT ME. Mouth agape. Wet leaves clinging to the bone in a luminescent stained-glass collage of putrefied colors. Bleached white from endless days ravaged by the sun, it stood out ominously from the leaf litter not far from the pity-stricken tree. Peering up to the heavens with hollowed mournful eyes, the expression it clung to was agonizing to me. What memory remained etched in the white of its face, I could not know. I didn't want to know as I stared at that fleshless hunk of bone.

SNAP!

If this wood were a church, I could only hope that the heavens had heard the tortured lament of this, the humiliated embodiment of a once humble servant.

Where was his God then?

Glowering down from the heavens, maybe, silent and unaffected, rattling those chains in chastisement. How many bad decisions did it take to form the construct of those chains? Each link a mislaid plan, a lasting regret, a false memory, a moment of overbearing pride, maybe, or an insecurity given weight to shape the future? If he had only known, would he have lived his life differently? Would he have made the choices offered him wisely? His flesh now hanging from ragged bone. How would he have lived his life if the true weight of those chains hadn't been unknown?

Everyone gets the feeling of déjà vu from time to time, so in that respect, I am just like everyone else. Where normality slipped silently away from me was when I discovered, in the hospital, that my time travel experiences were more than just sleepwalking. Everything in my mind is thin. Thin layers on top of layers on top of layers. There is nothing in my tangled thoughts strong enough for me to hold on to. Not even the disconcerting knowledge that I have been here before, in this very moment, gives me any relief.

I don't remember how I got here. I never remember the twisted path nor do I remember the how or the why, and I never will, but I'm sitting on a street bench, barefoot, again, the shadow of the station house looming behind me. My shoes, covered in dry forest debris and animal feces, are in the trunk of my car, wrapped in a plastic bag so they won't stink. Yes, I keep a box of plastic bags in my car. The occasional need for them, and gaffer tape, happens more often than you think. So now I sit on this splintered, poor excuse for a street bench, and my feet still stink, but that is perfectly fine with me.

The street is crowded with people walking about. Fine clothes. Cars moving along to the dictates of the traffic lights. Gleaming shop windows, polished to a beckoning shine. Stoops are being swept of litter by disgruntled and gloomy people, as if the day had defeated them as well.

Sometimes I sit on this bench, imagining that I want to know life. Not merely acknowledgement, per se. I want to appreciate its mundane nuances in a more three-dimensional way. A more emotionally connected way, just like that woman grumpily sweeping. I do have the capacity to feel emotion. I know what I feel when I capture a rain drenched day, or a tree cast in shadow, or the endless abyss of a spider's web laden with dew in the purple rouge of dawn. I know what I feel when I look at the picture, while it's developing, but not when I am actually in the moment. I feel nothing then. *Silence and emptiness.* Just the echo of the shutter behind the lens of the camera. Maybe that's all I am, all I was meant to be. An echo. A hollow imprint left to torture the wind, calling out over and over again … to no one. No one hears me. I can't even hear myself think let alone hear myself scream. My soul has no resonance anymore. The world is void of my voice.

Thousands of idle feet trample the earth, and yet I hear nothing but silence. I don't know why. Maybe it's the monotony of their pace. No tap dance. No waltz. No tango. Just unimaginative plodding along. Vacant faces pass me by, their destination neither here nor there. Barely living … barely breathing.

The air is poison. Don't they know this?

I snap off a few quick photos. The butcher's boy. A blood-soaked apron. A group of churlish lads. Coins to be counted. Quarrels to be had. Balking at each other as they toss about rowdy boyhood humiliations while dragging a puppy behind them on a taut leash. A trio at the street corner. Don't Cross, the light flashes. A child. A Mother. Hands clasped. Tight. Like a clenched fist. Chins up to the sky, eyes faint and distant, lost in a daydream they each so desperately want to believe.

Belief is just an idea, I think. I need something more than a fleeting idea. More than just another day to get through, more than just another empty night to suffer by, and that need is growing. I can't tell exactly what it is, but there is something missing. *In me.* I can't really determine if this something is something I actually had and lost along the way, or if it is something I never had to begin with. Whatever it is, it's a wicked thing, and I feel its absence. I feel as if there isn't enough light to hold back the dark … not enough of me left to manage the shadows.

If I were to fall apart, if I were to succumb to the void and the creatures taking sanctuary in its gloom, would anyone even notice that I had gone? Would anyone try to save me? *Probably not.* We've all got wooden stakes and no hammers.

ITS SPIRIT IS ONE SPIRIT
The spirit of all spirits...
Your spirit.

8

Twenty-Four Seven

May 29, 1998 ... 1:00 PM

S tale booze, sweat, and tobacco. The local gentlemen's pub. It was not all that unusual for me to find myself here. At mid-afternoon, they really are the quietest places to have a drink, a drink to wash away the lackluster memories of the day. All the regulars squint when someone walks in. Not because it's someone like you, or someone like me. They don't notice shit like that. Not in this place. It's a junkyard sinkhole with fancy neon. I liked to sit here in the dim light and stare through all the oddly shaped glass at the mural of Acapulco on the wall behind the bar. I don't know, the place has sort of a death row appeal to it. Everybody's just putting in their time, waiting it out in the dark. Not like those snooty grass-fed dilettantes with their jetliner smiles and their natural light, fresh flowers, and diplomatic *Bombay Sapphire* martinis. We, the sinkhole people, lack the palate for that sort of thing. We prefer the toxic shit served straight up by an atheist hooker in gold lamé pants who goes by the name Penny Chic. When she could say her name without coughing up a hunk of phlegm, that is. That's how we swallow it down. It isn't glamorous, but if you've fallen off the beaten path, or you've just been beaten off the path, this is as good a place as any to end up. It's a place where you can just sit a spell in silence and listen to the rustling of imaginary palm fronds in the balmy imaginary wind.

This was my kind of place, as I was acquainted with all of the table dancers by name. Real name that is. I had photographed many of them for modeling portfolios. Cameras are generally not allowed, but for me, it's just good business, for the establishment, for the dancers, and for the art form itself. The pub appreciated the publicity, the girls could afford my rates, but it was purely an artistic endeavor for me. Raw sexuality seems to come alive in black and white. The right angles. The dim, temperamental lighting, and the play of light and shadow across the sumptuous curve of a lanky thigh, the arch of a back, or the languid lilt of a smooth shoulder. There is nothing like a body stopped mid-motion. It is the sublime poetry of an artistically composed photograph, and these bodies were divine artistry in the flesh.

I don't know what draws men to places like this. That point of view seems sleazy to me, so you will have to ask a man to explain the reasoning behind his desire to gawk.

I am sure it is, in small part, the desire to admire something beautiful; though for most men, I doubt it is an artistic inclination. A feral one might be more accurate.

I threw the dancer a twenty and shot off a roll of film on her before she could even retrieve it.

This wasn't a sideshow. No blight on the neighborhood. It was a typical gentlemen's pub, despite my rather derogatory adjectives to the contrary. Proper. Stylish. It had it all. The effortless luxury of leather and burnished mahogany. The commanding weight of the glassware. Lighting so low that even the most purposeful mixture of desire and shame could be held in silent and secret restraint. Later in the evening, this place would be humming with activity. Fashionably dressed men would arrive in droves, singly and in groups, seeking relief from the day's stressors amidst the comforting haze of tobacco smoke, the thirst quenching bottomless glasses of stout ales and whiskey chasers, and the easy seduction of bared flesh. All for them, and the price made no difference, for this is the closest that they will ever come to having their own personal harem. An experience obviously well worth the shame.

The bartender brought my drink. Whiskey and soda. His name was Sven, and he served the less than savory clientele with a detached sense of apathy and contempt. A beautiful specimen of manhood he was, as Nordic as his namesake, with perfect musculature, skin slick with testosterone, a severely chiseled and handsome face, and a casual smile that could disarm even the most sinister of characters. Slap an animal pelt on him and you would swear you were looking at Erik the Red. All that Viking power was enough to send any woman careening into a moist faint. A perfect specimen. Perfectly lovely in every gentle gesture he made. Too bad he was perfectly homosexual. Didn't matter though, from where I was sitting, the view was captivating, and he seemed to be enjoying the fact that I was enjoying him. Too bad it couldn't last…

At my elbow, a scrubby flea-bitten wretch knocked over my drink as he reached for the ashtray in front of me. With one thousand others littering the bar top there really was no reason for him to invade my personal space. His ruse was feeble, stupid, annoying, and well beyond the limit of my patience. I gave him nothing more than a look of disdain as I quickly lifted my camera to avoid the whiskey dribble running towards me over the bar top.

He offered to purchase another drink for me.

I declined his offer rudely enough that any doubt regarding my availability should have been eradicated. I saw no reason to be polite. Encouraging such a despicable example of base manhood was not on my list of things to do. However, his capacity for understanding was obviously limited. Drooling, he inched towards me, and I feared that this would digress into one of two scenarios. Under normal circumstances, I would have been prepared for both, but I had left my mace in the car, not that it would have deterred the likes of this fecal-stained animal anyway, but my utter lack of mindfulness pissed me all the way off. My ass cheeks clenched the stool as he inched closer, so I braced myself for the inevitable altercation.

"Lesbian," he exhaled in a slurred whisper.

At least he wasn't monosyllabic, and actually, many of the ladies who danced here were, in fact, lesbians, and considering this perverted human puke-stain, I am sure it was a relief. For them. At least they would never feel the need for a shower afterwards. His stink made me want to gag, so I was not even going to take any sort of courteous tack in my response. I practically barked directly into his face, "You fucking wish, then at least you could walk out of here still feeling like a man. Now get your fat, pig-sweating ass out of my face."

He growled, slammed his empty glass down, threw some money onto the bar, and then left the premises in a surly state of offence. He attempted a parting shot on his way out the door. It was nothing but incoherent gibberish. *What a spanner.* I had offended him, go figure. I would have a laugh over that later in the evening, but at that moment, the adrenalin rush had forced my shoulders well up over my ears.

I ordered another whiskey and soda.

When it arrived, I took a huge gulp of it and then slowly exhaled through my mouth. Sean, this afternoon's premier dancer, smiled at me. A maudlin smile, conferring a look of womanly gratitude. I raised my glass to her. Thanks to me, she wouldn't have to endure his hungry eyes gnawing at her flesh for the remainder of her shift.

My temperament, rough and uncompromising on occasion, compelled me to assist. I have no problem with men appreciating women. Conversely, when appreciation turns to salivating reptilian depravity, I have to draw the line. It's all about the principles of common decency really. The men who frequent pubs like this in the middle of the afternoon are not the amiable sort you would normally wish to engage. They are not the trimmed, pressed, heavy-tipping businessmen who arrive at the workday's end. They are generally not any sort of proper man at all. Emasculating them is a delight. Show no fear, and they're stripped of their power. Even so, it looked like the peace and quiet I had hoped to find would elude me again. Sven ambled down the bar and set another drink in front of me, one that I didn't remember asking for. He smiled and shifted his glance towards the other end of the bar, indicating that I should momentarily acknowledge the piercing stare leveled in my direction, one that sought to impale me. *Where do they come from, these wraiths of humanity?*

"No rest for the weary," Sven chided me under his breath.

"No rest even for the dead," I replied.

As I watched the stranger approach, I felt something foul and oppressive hit the base of my spine, and everything went grey. I could feel the icy perspiration on my forehead, and this only increased my discomfort. I fought for a rationalization, a circumstance, something that might define what I was feeling. I had grappled with many a ruffian in my day without even the slightest hesitation, but this man set me into a state of unease I wasn't at all familiar with. There was something off about him. I swallowed hard to keep down the lump of anxiety that had risen rather determinedly in my throat.

He didn't know what sort of person I was. *Probably didn't care.* Was he curious about me, a woman patron in a strip club? *No, of course not.* It was desire. He was dazed with it more than likely. He had needs, like all men do. Appetites and cravings better indulged solo, in my opinion.

His eyes never left me as he moved closer, despite the sway of the dancing girl offering the promise of herself. It was only a promise, after all. I was real. Real, smoldering, and alive. But there were barstools and an endless sea of empty glasses between us. A whole world of agony between us, drowned in the backwash. Yet he seemed unaffected and navigated the distance with a deliberate long-stridden grace — lithe and sinewy — eyes focused on me with fierce concentration.

He sat down beside me.

I gave him the customary once over. He looked decent enough, dressed in dark jeans and a denim jacket. The cuffs of a plain white shirt were visible at his wrists. He took a pack of cigarettes out of his pocket, tapped it a few times against the bar top, and then lit one without hurrying. He smoked silently for a moment, his long blonde hair falling in feathered wisps against his face. He turned his head towards me, exhaled, and smiled at me. He had luminous and reflective grey-blue eyes. Eyes the color of mercy. "Don't often see a lass in a place like this," was all he said to me, and I thought, *Bravo*. Yet another cliché pickup line.

Considering the depth and intensity of his smile, I had expected something a bit more stylish, but as I have said before, expectations only lead to disappointment, but the question did warrant some pondering. Why would I come to place like this? For the illusion of it maybe; after all, that is why the girls dance. They feel protected by it, empowered by it.

My silence didn't seem to deter him.

"Let me see your palm," he asked, but his tone had changed. It had become a little harsh and insistent.

I threw back my whiskey before I asked, "Which one?" and then I picked up my pack of cigarettes and my lighter. Sven shot me a quick look of disapproval, but I wasn't in the mood to have one our classic silent disputes. I didn't need his permission to have a conversation with such an interesting patron, there were so few, so I ignored his impassioned look of concern and lit up. I took a deep drag from the cigarette and anxiously waited as the stranger mulled over his options.

"Both," he continued, accepting the rules of the game, but in reality, this seemingly playful interaction wasn't really a game at all, and I sensed from the blush on his face that he knew it as well. "Are you left handed or right?"

"Both," I replied.

There is nothing more stimulating than forcing someone into a corner. It's tantamount to taking them hostage. Could they maintain the ruse? How would they play the next hand? Would the words stumble upon their tongue, and would subtle deceptive gestures reveal concealed intent. The telling twitch of an eye, perhaps. The wetting of a parched lower lip. I made no attempt to hide my amusement. After all the things I had seen, a game of cat and mouse hardly seemed cruel. I met his stare and held it for ransom, but I remained silent.

At once, his face flashed of crimson. Apparently, my antagonistic yet flirty thrust had been accurate. Eagerly awaiting his parry, I took another drag from my cigarette and held out my left hand, which he took rather forcefully, but then his face softened as he looked at the faint lines and indentations, smoothing them out with his thumbs. His flesh in contact with mine made me cringe.

However soft and loving his touch might have seemed, with each caress, my palm ached as if ten thousand tiny pins had been hammered into my skin. He acknowledged my obvious discomfort with a reserved yet pointed smile.

I felt a little dizzy, and as he held my hand, sharp imaginings began flooding my mind. *I want to fuck him.* Then I am. Atop the bar like a crazed banshee, my hair whipping in the torrent of the overhead fan, his body writhing, slick like a serpent, beneath the punishing blows of my hips.

I knew that my pulse had risen to a maddening pace. I felt it smashing at my temples and crashing in my ears like waves of thunder. An aggressive heat had consumed my body, and I felt the tingling sensation of static in my hand, thrusting me out of my waking dream back into reality. I could see his lips moving. "What?" I blurted out like a dimwit.

"This is how you were," he repeated.

But for the rigid intensity of his expression, I almost laughed out loud in an infantile attempt to regain my composure. Voodoo charlatans rate highly on my list of light entertainment, and although I might have been able to contain the anxious laughter, I couldn't contain a bit of well-mannered pithiness, "Really … you don't say … what about now?"

As I replaced my left hand with my right, biting pinpricks of electricity surged through my fingertips again. He grimaced this time, and yawning lines of fear tore across his face, drawing out deep creases around his mouth and eyes. An awkward silence prevailed while he gathered his bearings. "You see monstrous things," he whispered in a hushed and secretive breath, almost as if he were revealing some sinful character flaw I possessed, and my mouth filled with warm spit. I debated whether or not I should tell him of the headless flesh pile I had seen earlier that day. *No.* No sense frightening a stranger. Not this stranger anyway. He seemed harmless, innocent. I had frightened enough men in my life, some strangers, some not. Their fright comforted me, kept me distant, and distance was all I really wanted in life. A good safe distance. "All day every day," I replied. "So, by karmic default, does that make me a monster?"

As he released my hand, I noticed that his was shaking, and I felt a little guilty for my smugness. I looked away, searching for the appropriate apology, which, for some asinine reason, I thought might be at the bottom of my whiskey glass. It wasn't, so I proceeded with, "I'm sorry. I should get hazard pay. My job. It makes me less agreeable than most women…" I didn't look at him when I said it. I just kept on fiddling with the empty glass, my words trailing off into the atmosphere on a loose wisp of smoke. I finally looked up when the silence became unbearable, and we exchanged forlorn glances. His eyes had become serious. I wasn't sure if it was anger or sympathy, and it gave me start. Confusion smashed into me, but I wanted to continue our conversation, despite the sense of apprehension and against my better judgment, but the words just clattered about in my head like loose rusty nails when a sharp pain hit me behind my eyes, and I couldn't seem to make any sense of the muddled desire I felt. Desire I wasn't supposed to be entertaining for a stranger. That fluid sense of dread, slick with erotic imaginings of deviant and delicious sexual dramatics and equally deviant and delicious climactic dénouements.

It only takes a momentary lapse of sanity for a person to hurl themselves into a dangerous situation. I knew this, had witnessed the grisly consequences often enough, but at that moment, even though my logic mind was stealthily kicking me in the shins, it wouldn't have taken much of a lapse at all. I fancied that he made love like a deranged bloodthirsty freak, that he could break and torture my body and my will, and that he could devour me so wholly and completely, I'd be enslaved for eternity and wouldn't care. Thinking of my own submission, I writhed perversely in my seat, legs trembling, and I could feel the hot irons of desire branding the skin of my inner thighs. His beautiful mouth implored me, silently and urgently. I wanted to savor the wet of his lips ... and I wanted him to rip my soul from my body and tear my flesh to bits.

Suddenly, the telephone rang, distracting me. Sven dove like a trapeze artist towards the end of the bar and answered it with a contrived cheery businesslike tone in an attempt to conceal the underlying irritation and disappointment he felt. Apparently, he had been as enchanted with the stranger as I was.

The stranger.

When I found myself again and turned to face him, he was gone, and yet, I could still feel the warmth of his hand. I felt tainted. I felt ashamed. I felt as if I had been touched by the damned.

ALL THAT WAS DARK IS NOT FORSAKEN.

9

Poetry *and the Country House*

June 6, 1998, give or take a reluctant hour or two.

I t was a sun-scorched top-down sort of day. Optimistic breezy clouds caught the wind and fluttered effortlessly over the hedgerows, and the air was filled with the scent of dew lying over newborn flowers. Summer was almost upon us. The sky was clear and blue and beautiful, and for once, everything seemed on the threshold of something better. I felt romantic. I felt willowy, fickle, and love-struck. I felt like cuddling up against Killy, and I felt like putting some trendy youth-in-revolt pop music on the radio, opening the bottle of gin next to me, having a slug or two, and then falling into a deep, dreamless sleep as we drove to the country house,

strong suit. I felt as equally uncomfortable in fancy dress as I did in this house as I tripped and stumbled my way into the foyer, which was wastefully large and lofty, rising up to the third story of the house, and ending with an impressive stained-glass skylight. The sun glittered down through the multicolored panes of glass and cast a kaleidoscope of flickering light on the acres of drab tapestries, which hung from the walls as remnants of ghostly bygone eras. Eras of splendor and irredeemable pretense. That pretense clung to everything, even the musty stagnant air. I felt trapped. I felt my soul weeping for the loss of light.

Heavy drapes hung from every window as if the sunlight were an affront to the house's very existence, so Killy had to stop every few minutes or so to switch on the lights as we made our way through a maze of dark passages, which were cluttered with antique furniture that had been left covered in linen sheets, thereby reduced to earthbound phantoms. Yes, the ambiance was oppressive, and I felt terribly out of place, almost unworthy. Killy knew it, too. He just smiled at me, said nothing, and merrily dragged the luggage behind him.

We ended our journey in a small library off the master bedroom on the second floor. Warm and close, the mahogany and leather offered solace, the scent of the old books offered calm, and the words of the old poets offered sanctuary. He also knew that if I was going to feel comfortable enough to engage him sexually, this would be the only suitable room in the house. He let the luggage drop haphazardly to the floor and then made to make a fire. I asked for whiskey and then announced my intention to take a hot bath. He gave me a grin and said that he would unpack while I bathed, so I kicked off my shoes and then made my way to the bathroom.

My muscles were stiff from the lengthy road trip and could do with a warm soak. As I walked into the room though, I came to realize that comfort and ease wouldn't be an issue. For a shitter, the bathroom was no drab common convenience. It was nothing less than virgin marble splendor. A sumptuous doom poured from the gilded taps, and I felt self-conscious undressing, as if my naked humility might tarnish the dignity of the room. *I don't belong here.* Everything including the floor knew this, but I couldn't give in so soon, and so I tried to step arrogantly into the grandness of it all.

Candles lit, toes wet, I smoked a cigarette while watching the balmy water glimmer in the warm flickering light. Bath oils slicked the water's surface and scented the air as sumptuous clouds of steam rose from my breasts, mingling with the smoke left off my lips. The tub was surrounded by mirrors, and I found it difficult to resist the seduction. I hadn't touched myself in a very long time, so I closed my eyes, slipped down into the water, and sank into a selfish moment of sublime ecstasy. I might have only been happier if I had drowned.

By the time I had finished, Killy had a roaring fire going. I entered the room, leaving the silk robe open, as my body was still damp. He told me to sit by the fire and dry myself off in its warmth. This seemed like a pleasant and thoughtful suggestion, so I obeyed. Once I was comfortable, he knelt in front of me and put one hand between my legs. With the other, he handed me a glass of whisky and a couple of pills.

"Things are so much better when you're calm," he

said with the abrupt and weighty articulation of a doctor, as if I had a particular affliction, which could be traced back to some logical Jungian or Freudian subconscious origin, one in which alcohol and sedatives would undoubtedly cure. I noticed the rosy-red blush on his skin, the razor-sharp sparkle in his eyes, and his silken hair, the waywardness of it, its delicate texture as it fell over his forehead when he leaned into me. But behind the intoxicatingly boyish façade, there was nothing but a brute, a fiend, fed on obsession and desire. He knew how to tempt me, knew only one modest caress would set me on the verge of madness. With his smile, any hope I had of salvation flew away into little burning embers, just like those from the fire, flickering for an instant and then cooling to nothing more than bits of dust and ash. It frightened me — how he could dominate me so — but I was too tired to attempt a series of feeble and futile struggles to overcome his will. I took up the glass of whiskey and swallowed the pills.

He then proceeded to caress me, almost tenderly, but not quite. He swooned over how beautiful my flesh looked in the light of the fire, how its rouge favored me, how he wanted to dance across it like a flame. How he wanted to "scar and burn it."

As his sadistic endearments stretched their lies across my mind, I felt weak and a little dizzy. The whiskey was taking affect, and I felt like I was slowly moving out of myself, settling into the flowing black depths of the nothingness that was us, and the clock ticked, loudly on the wall as hot air from the fire ruffled his hair. I looked into his eyes, detached, impersonal, and my own were reflected back into me. My hopelessness and my indifference. I spread my legs so that he might look at me. He licked his lips, mouth glistening, moist and inviting. He put his hands on my knees, angled my legs wider, lifted my left leg up over the arm of the chair. Then he leaned in and kissed me. Still wet from the bath, it felt delicious. *Vile. Depraved Decadent.* He bit into me … harder … and again, and then he teased me gently with his tongue. I moaned as his polluted caresses travelled through my body, sending a filthy, repellent heat into my veins. I dropped the whiskey glass, threw my head back, resigned myself to submission, and the clock continued to tick. An endless corrosive ticking. Time neither gaining nor receding upon itself.

So it would be for the week. We would cross over and back again the fine line between torture and contentment. He read me poetry in hushed breath, doted on me to excess, and violated me with a sharpness unknown to all except a hard-hearted killer.

For a respite and to nurse my tender wounds, we went for long walks along the cliffs, the swirling waters of the sea churning beneath us. For hours we would walk, as the sea scarred and battered the rocks below. We walked … and we walked, until the sky grew grey and the bedrock quaked and moaned as the sea shifted with distant impending storms. I would shield my eyes against the sun as it peered in luminous shards through the gusting mass of clouds, and as my feet edged the rocky precipice, I would lean into the wind, throwing my arms out freely to the tempest to come, its impetuous fury nearly lifting me from my feet. I could feel the earth slipping beneath me. Could feel the pebbles of reason and rationality slipping away, neglected and forgotten. It was like gazing upon a great abyss at the edge of the universe, an emptiness beyond redemption and beyond faith.

As my body relaxed, Killy would ease me with gentle persuasion closer to the edge, and then in an instant, he would catch my arm and pull me back, always uttering the same inexplicable vagaries as he did so, the usual patronizing sternness of his voice turning for a moment to an almost sincere cry of distress. I could almost hear the tears behind his words. "Rowan, you are exasperating. I don't know whether to love you, rape you, or slit your fucking throat."

I was certain, at times, he wished to do all three.

There was no escaping him or this miserable place.

We never left the estate, not even for a meal. Of course, I was as much to blame for that as he. I didn't like restaurants or being in public. That was just my nature. Both were far too ostentatious and formal for my tastes. I felt much more relaxed and comfortable at home, cooking or otherwise. Mostly otherwise. I couldn't cook. Couldn't boil water without some dire kitchen catastrophe. I can't visualize anything in motion, but Killy can. Killy, in contrast, is a spectacular cook. Where he had acquired such a skill, I had no idea. Didn't care either. His precision with a blade and hunk of raw meat was a frightening spectacle.

We gorged ourselves every night of the week. Fresh fish and vegetables; succulent scallops and raw oysters; roast chicken breast marinated in herbs, cut straight from the garden. Every night he prepared feasts fit for a queen, served upon porcelain contempt, and properly accompanied by expensive wine from his private reserves.

It was all so delicious that I chewed with my mouth open, loudly, ignorantly, spitting bits of food across the table at him. I practically choked on it as if every meal were my last, all while guzzling the wine straight out of the bottle. How pleasant and quaint everything seemed by candlelight, how wonderful when everything fit together so nicely. Killy often said that we fit together nicely. He was a sly, deceitful one, trying to exploit my weaknesses, my kindness, and most of all, my love, and it was working, well, almost working. *I knew what he was. I knew what he'd done.*

When night fell, the shadows would gather in that same candlelight, haunting the walls and ceilings like gothic marionettes, taunted into grotesque and loathsome postures by some phantom death master. As they whirled about the room, I would lie in bed, tossing and turning, my overheated body searching for relief amidst the coolness of silk. Across the room by the fire, Killy would sit contented in his armchair, glasses perched precariously on his nose, the smoke from his cigar aggravating the air above his head as he perused his collection of obscure and savage poetry. Once, when my weary eyes found and rested upon him in the dark, I came to realize that the space between us was insurmountable.

Often in that same darkness, he would lift his sullen voice to me and ask, "Do you need something, Rowan?" knowing full well that I often thought rather carelessly of my needs.

Yes, Killy, I need a tourniquet … to stop my soul bleeding.

I could never really let go with him. I always felt that he was prying into my mind somehow, pushing against my defenses all the time, and aligning himself with the fears I revealed to no one. He could read the subtle transcripts of my subconscious mind like he were purchasing my most secreted thoughts and desires as if he were ordering from a fancy French menu. His tenderness was no more than cold-hearted bribery. His lies, covered with promises. There was a price to pay for his kindness, so high a price. When we made love, if you could call it that, the only thoughts I had were that of suicide.

I barely existed in his world. I was an idea of an idea. With him, my unhappiness seemed endless, my despair, transcendent, and each day as they passed, I found myself drifting further and further away from reality. I resigned myself to nothingness, as my want for his cruelty grew steadily worse. With each brutal kiss, each merciless and vicious embrace, I succumbed willingly, completely, to the sickness in him. *I was getting close.* Eventually, I would cross the threshold into a terrifying darkness; one I wished no release from, for his was a darkness as hollow as my own.

He was my salvation, my undoing.

He knew just the right words to say and precisely when to say them, and when he whispered them to me, he did so as if he meant it. Vicariously, we lived and died in each other arms. For every part of me that desired him, there was another distant, darker part that recoiled in disgust.

I felt no love for him. It was more ecstatic absolution. Through him, I remained free from the guilt I had felt as long as I could remember. His touch — a punishment I lacked the courage to inflict upon myself. When we bled, the crimson in our blood tasted the same. Scrap metal. He tasted of salt and lithium grease, and he smelled of flux and butane. He had once said to me, "A penny for your thoughts, Rowan," and that's how it is for me when I think of him. A bit of copper wire on my tongue.

We feed on each other,

Gnaw on each other.

That's the essence of us, pure and simple, and the only poetry is that of my hatred for him.

ALL THAT IS DEAD IS NOT FORGOTTEN.

10

Visions *of Buttercups*

June 15, 1998, relieved.

I switched off my mobile and slipped into the tedium of the drive ahead. It was a deliriously high climbing country road, like so many others I had dreamt of. It would be a long, uninspiring ride, but I was thankful for the solitude. An isolated week in the country with Killy was more than my mind and my body could stand. In returning to work, I somehow felt the uncluttered promise of fulfillment again.

I glanced out the open window at the far-reaching blue sky. Out here, away from the city's sooty architecture, it seemed immense and endless, yet so close. Not a sound to distract me, other than the droning of the car engine, I let my mind wander off into a daydream. A daydream of a field at night. A warm night, swathed in a velvety blanket of flickering stars. Everything was still, except for the whisper of the breeze against the grasses, and there was someone with me. Beside me. Stretched out like a lanky weed in the tall grass. For a moment, when the moon slipped out from beneath the grey veil of clouds, I could almost make out his face in the darkness. His eyes shimmered as brilliantly as the stars, and his smile reflected the gentle melancholy of the moon. I could feel the touch of his hand, his slender fingers entangled in mine, and as the countryside rushed past me at high speed, I felt an ache somewhere in the depths of my soul, blurring my thoughts to the point I almost missed the roadblock ahead of me. I hit the brakes, and my car skidded to a sideways stop in the gravel along the side of the road. I took me a moment to shake my head clear of the dust, and when I realized where I was, my stomach twisted in on itself. Surrounding me was an endless sea of sunshine. Held in its sway, I could see everywhere. I could see everywhere I had ever been in that vast field of swaying grasses. Sun kissed with buttercups as far as the eye could see.

We were running, always running.
Rhys with his shoelaces undone,
Stumbling,
Arms flailing in the warm summer wind.
He never tied his shoelaces,
And he was always stumbling.
He would stumble over me, tumble into me,
Sending both of us to the ground,
Giggling and rolling aimlessly
Through the buttercups.

"I'll show you mine, if you show me yours?"

I had a summer frock on that day, faintly flowered, with little blue periwinkles cascading over a butter cream yellow background. It was so thin and billowed willfully in the breeze as I raised it up for him.

I kissed his cheek.

He kissed my breast.

I could feel the heat of his mouth through the filmy fabric, and as I twisted myself against him, he moved his hands up underneath the lace. The thatch felt warm and prickly, and the scent of him, of honey mingled with the dew and the perfume of faraway flowers, fell faint on my lips. "Can I kiss it?" he asked, and I just smiled at him.

His lips trembled against me.

And I trembled into the blue of the sky.

The sun felt warm as it played softly over the grasses and tenderly over our bodies that day. The sun, artist and architect, praised us that day, painting us into that beautiful buttercup field. Our innocence, our love for one another fashioned sparkling crystalline tears of joy on every flower petal and every blade of grass.

A thousand summers ago, it seemed. One we were. I'd tasted freedom that day, lost in eternity's brilliance, and I'd lost the will to breathe. Was it love that had surrounded me so closely that day? Was it love that had embraced so completely my innocent soul, or was it nothing more than the sun in my eyes, or a clever dream?

Rhys ... He never tied his shoelaces.

I remember now ... This was *my* buttercup field.

I couldn't believe it, and I almost doubled over with laughter. I wanted to run, fling my arms out wide, throw my head back, and revel in the wistful enchantment that was desperately inching to the surface, but I hesitated, because I was a fool. Fairy tales have this power over our lives. We desperately want the illusion of a happily ever after. Despite the inevitable carnage, we hope for that with all our hearts and souls, but those fairy tales, their illusions are nothing more than trickery. Vile and distasteful artifice. They lie silent in the shadows, waiting to betray you when you need most to believe in them. *Foolishness.* It's all nothing but foolish childhood shit.

I got out of the car, stretched the muscles in my legs and in my mind, strapped on my gear, and took off down the path, but I wasn't running, stumbling, or otherwise through the soaring grasses and yellow flowers. I was trudging, marching towards eminent doom. Eventually, it was there before me, just up ahead. The vague, darkened form of something, lying in a low thicket. I can see it now. So close I can almost touch it. Flayed open at the breast. Cartilage gleaming in the sun. Pale sinewy flesh. Skin stripped aside. A tangle of ligatures decorating the neck like a fanciful bow on a child's birthday gift. I knelt down and leaned over the body for a closer look, and it was a girl who looked back at me. She was very young; doubtfully she was much older than I had been when I first experienced the innocent pleasures of this field. On the other hand, my memory of this place wasn't of the same tone and texture, and that fact was made brutally apparent by the strange yet almost alluring combination of sex and death reflected in her dead distant eyes, as she lay there, almost in tranquil repose, at the side of the riverbank. The macabre peacefulness of her face betraying the silent consequence. Covered with mud and debris, she had been cast aside, no more than refuse amongst a mosaic of discarded newspapers, tin cans, and black ooze.

I felt the bile rise up in my throat.

What's wrong with me?

This was nothing. Nothing special. Nothing miraculous or extraordinary. Nothing I hadn't seen a million times before, and yet, I felt stricken with despair. The memory of my buttercup field had now been corrupted. I paused over the body for long moments between shots as each image burned itself into my retinas.

Questions, there were always so many questions…

Had she come here with her poet lover? Wandered here? Wandered far from an endless darkness? Had she sought this place for all its hope and promise, or had she been dragged here under the pretense of redemption? What did he take from her as he gnawed on her flesh, as he clawed at her chastity? He took more than just her life. Did she cry out under a bloated moon that night? Beg maybe. Did she beg for mercy as he cut into her, as he offered her entrails as sacrifice to that demon moon?

Although the sun had eradicated its treachery, the moon had hung low in the sky that night, dull, crimson, and bloated, cleaved by jagged cloud and mist. The mental image set my mind spinning with sinister thoughts. Words tumbled from mind to lip. Melancholy words I could not place: *'The victims have all been bled.'* With those unspeakable words swirling around in my head, I walked the scene for a minute, searching for the Inspector in charge, and at each step, as if they had heard the words too, the composure drifted away on the faces of each officer in turn.

The youngest of them leaned forward in an unsuccessful attempt to move the body for an improved look. As he did so, a piece of her flesh tore loose from her wrist like milk soaked crepe paper. He stepped back with a jerk, shaking the horror from his hand as her arm fell to the ground. Its impact sounded of a dead fish slopping into a bucket of mud. I waited for the horror to take hold of him, but aside from his skin taking on the tint of a stained sheet, to my surprise, he hid the disgust well, chewing on his lower lip in a futile attempt to repress his emotions. Unfortunately for me, my internal organs refused to retain their composure. The tea and dry toast I had eaten that morning freed themselves from my stomach in a brutally sadistic purge.

One might suppose that vomiting is a bad thing. The razor wire unfurling in the abdomen. The flood of acid forcing its way upward, eating away at the sinewy stretch of your esophagus. The metallic taste of blood and bile on your tongue, and then the convulsive force as you reject the lining of your own stomach. No. It isn't such a bad thing at all. Having vomited up my contempt, I felt like a new woman, so I spit a few times to clear the chunks from my mouth, dragged my shirtsleeve across my lips, and then readjusted myself. Stripped of any lingering reservations or distress, I dashed about the scene like a possessed nutter with a smile and a purpose. Everything went quickly, and nothing seemed to bother me in the slightest. Everyone had seen me retching in the weeds, so I didn't have to waste any energy on emotional artifice. My revulsion had become blurred and indistinct like the sun, this field, and every single flower in it, so I tore myself out of the gloom and got to work. What difference does the blinding fury of death make to me? I can look full on into the abyss and not wince. I have always been able to do that.

11

Clarity

6:00 PM, state of dementia.

S omehow, even though my legs felt as if I had borrowed them from a week-old corpse, I managed to slog through the remainder of the day, but the distance between my mind and soul had expanded with each passing hour from a mildly irritating fissure into a bleak chasm. I had supper with Killy. One of those fancy French places: heavy chintz draperies, ridiculously delicate glassware, and a wait staff who served snobbery for an appetizer more slippery than the escargot. It was all shiny shoes and even shinier smiles, ready to implode at the slightest bourgeois suggestion. *Snips, snails, and puppy dogs tails all in a light wine sauce.* I can't remember what we ate or what trite and inconsequential conversation we might have assaulted each other with. The entire night had congealed into a grey slurry of tastelessness, and it dragged on endlessly. Present company made the evening no less painful. Killy sat there. Pensive mood. Smartly dressed. The usual solemn and proper black tie, loose around his neck, but knotted with killer precision and the expensive platinum cufflinks, glinting arrogantly from beneath the sleeves of his divine Dolce suit. He looked up at me, and I flinched. His face was familiar and yet strange in all its little insignificant details. His jet-black eyes gleamed brightly in the faux romantic candlelight as he chewed on his bloody steak without mercy, gristle and bits of raw flesh decorating his smile. Much like the expensive wine we were drinking, his emotions were always well decanted. Robust yet smooth with the aftertaste of petrol. Beneath the suave veneer was a monster waiting to be fed. I found it difficult to look at him, so I focused on the perspiration from the wine glass as it slid down the lanky crystal stem and dripped onto my hand. It was as chill as my heart as it slipped slowly over the exposed veins of my wrist like a tiny, penitent teardrop. *Drowning one's sorrows.* I could see then why that phrase was so poignant. Two glasses of wine. Killy hit me with a sharp glance and smiled at me. Maybe it would take three.

Dr. Killkhenny was a master illusionist, and I was convinced that I was the only one who saw the deception. The only one who knew what he was and what he could do. Frightfully expensive meal aside, he would still be hungry. Would still feel a savage craving, the raw meat and the wine having merely intensified his need for human flesh. He would have mine before the night's end. Of that, there was no doubt.

Despite the pills and the liquor, which Killy has ever at the ready, I never really feel at ease anywhere or with anyone. I lie to myself and go through the motions, but calm in the sense of being comfortable is a foreign thing to me. I never feel calm like that, not even when I should be able to relax, in my own home, surrounded by all the stupid little things that define me as a person. This is when I invariably realize that I don't know myself as a person at all. I dare anyone to find comfort in that. So I just sit in the dark. Manic thoughts — cutting and disjointed — racing through my mind, and I can't even remember a single thing about my life as a moment before this moment. The whims of youth, the fickle laughter, the carefree barefoot days by a cool shaded pond. I know I lived such moments. All those stock and trade blushes, giggles, and shy smiles cast away on wind-blown petals. I know those moments exist somewhere for me, somewhere beyond the dark, but all I can remember is that all my disappointments about love and life began there, in that murky place. Killy says I dissociated. I made a choice, but I don't think so. Something was taken from me then, or maybe I lost it on my own. Nevertheless, this something is missing, along with most memories of it. I do have a childhood, but I don't know where to begin with it. It's become abstracted and unrecognizable to me. Everything is weird and blurry and painful, masked by an inexplicable darkness. Sticky and viscous with decay. Impenetrable. It wraps itself around and around me until everything I think I might be able to feel suffocates to death. Even if I could come to terms with it, have an honest opinion of it, I would never be comfortable with it fully. That said, I would at least be willing to tolerate it.

For clarity, I would tolerate anything.

I get up out of bed and go to the window. I had left it open, deliberately, and I can feel the gentle breeze, stealing through the opening, as I hoped it would, bringing with it the scent of sea air. I feel isolated from myself as the taste of salt hits my tongue. It stings a little, justifying all of my anxiety about everything. I look down on the street. The glow of the street lamps illuminates a city in the heavy-handed grip of sleep. There's nothing out there but the moon, and the lack of sound is oppressive. *The silent death of the light mourning the loss of color.* That's how the memories come to me now. In puddles from an early evening rain, littering dirty streets. The moon hovering over them as they draw down its bitter light. Their shimmering onyx surfaces reflecting its discontent. In a thousand shades of grey, reflecting its hubris, its lies.

I turn and have a quick look around my living room. It looks a shambles. Smothered in dust and ruin, it looks the picture of hysteria, unkempt and out of control. Bits and bobs and little meaningless trinkets lay about in various states of decay. A miserably ragged loveseat. A few antique tables, watermarked and scarred with cigarette burns from my carelessness. The imitation Persian rug fraying at the edges, pattern worn by the relentless pacing of restless soul. I don't sleep, and I don't really dream. Sometimes for weeks at a time. If I am not pacing the floor, then I lie in my bed and stare at the multicolored vortices that loop like a film reel on the backs of my eyelids. I do this just about every night, except for tonight. Tonight, I lie naked on the sofa, my hair wrapped in a towel, the crimson remunerations of Killy's transgressions still visible on my abdomen and hips. His sinister whispers still echoing in my ears.

"Tell me Rowan, tell me what he does to them. Tell me how he cuts them. How he feels when he tastes their blood."

It isn't so much that he wants to hear me say the words. No. He wants to see the panic and suffering behind my eyes as I struggle not to say them. He wants to feel the struggle. Wants to draw it out of me like an elixir. He's never known struggle, so he feeds on it — feeds on the poison in me.

Killy's lovemaking style is vicious. More of a paper cut to the soft skin between your fingers. A raw burn that takes forever to heal. It should be comforting in a way to know someone cares about me enough to inflict that kind of torture, but even in the throes of an excruciating orgasm, I can find no release, not enough to sleep anyway. I could get up and leave. Walk barefoot in the rain like I've done so often in the past. I always have that option, but with him, I feel like I can't move. That I have no will to move, so I lie there, the room and my ravaged flesh awash in that moon's sinister and secretive embrace. Again, sleep will not come, so while the hours recede into the past, I try to reason away the chill I feel in my blood.

It's merely the cool summer rains.

I know it's not the rain. My mind knows better than to wrap itself around a lie like that. Never a moment's rest, my own mind callously taunts me with useless logic, and tonight, even the tattered drapes taunt me as well, swaying fitfully in the moon's stale breath.

Killy emerges from the bedroom. Cast in shadow, he

stands like an inquisitor, leaning against the doorframe, arms crossed, searching for me earnestly through the darkness, but our glances don't hit upon each other for long. The faint flush on his chest and face, the way that smug smile of his catches the moonlight, and the rancid stench of sex still clinging to his flesh. He looks like the monster in the mirror at the cottage. The feral amusement in his eyes. I look away from him. Of one thing, I am certain. He disgusts me. It's shameful how he mocks me. Mocks love. Mocks passion. Mocks everything … even death. With Killy, I am bound to a debilitating state of self-loathing, and even if I'd wanted to, I've never been able to achieve his level of self-righteous depravity. I used to be able to match his coldness with a callousness of my own, but my defenses have slipped over the years, and I feel as if I have lost all control. I lift myself up onto the pillows and throw a blanket over me with haste.

"Come back to bed," he says abruptly, after having derided me with his silent gaze for a moment. "Come on, Rowan. Let me touch you some more. I'll be gentle. I promise."

He always lies when he makes promises, and even though I crave him when I'm feeling weak and alone, "I can't, and I won't," let him touch me.

No sooner had the refusal passed from my lips, he turned and made an agitated retreat. "Suit yourself then," came his last words from the darkness before he slammed the bedroom door. Seemed an odd thing for him to say to me. *Nothing in my life suits me, asshole, not even my own skin.*

12

A Person of Interest

July 22, 1998 till the cold came, yet again.

O ver the next few months, sobriety seemed to
have me stumbling through my life like a
degenerate buffoon. One moment I was
flooded with dread and shame, and the next, abandoned
idiotic exuberance. I hadn't had a drink or a pill in weeks.

The workload was a little lighter. A few car crashes. A
couple of gunshots to the head. A strangulation. A stab-
wound, or two or maybe three. A rather messy suicide.
The sense and restraint of rational humanity had been
reduced to scattered chunks, it seemed, and I felt like a
ticket taker at a carnival freak show, so I went various
places for drinks, caught a few black and white porn

flicks at the local perv palace, but mostly I just walked around without direction or purpose. I didn't seem to feel any murmurs of disquiet, and at least the pounding anxiety in my head had diminished since that day in the buttercup field. I was aware of very little to nothing, especially when it came to Killy, the shit bastard, whose insistence about our relationship had become more than an annoyance. I couldn't stand the sight of him, and holding a smile or any reasonable facsimile of for his benefit made my teeth hurt. I avoided him as much as I could, and with all this solitary time on my hands, my mind had acquired a distressing tendency to slip into the cobwebbed shadows more and more frequently thinking of Rhys. My first and only real love. It set my nerves on edge every time he popped into my head.

I had promised myself many times that I would stop fixating on him so obsessively. Killy postulated often that letting go of him would alleviate my affectedness, and I hated him more each time he mentioned it, even if the suggestion might have had some merit. He was a doctor after all, and so I made a few half-hearted attempts to indulge him, but each time I did, the haze would clear in my mind, and I would I realize that my life really had no meaning without Rhys haunting me.

That day on the bridge, I remember him just staring into the distance, into some private abyss, containing all of the darkness that could be known to a child. Pain, humiliation, and fear. For my own part at that moment, I felt that I was the beginning and the end of his misery. Then by force of will, or by force gravity, he plummeted from the bridge to his death. I remember how the crystalline waters of the stream broke across his fingertips, and how his wounds wept silent tears to be carried away with the tide. I remember it all so vividly now. I remember the look left on his dead face, twisted and bleeding on those rocks. I remember the innocence and the purity of it.

A still image.

A photograph.

A fleck of glossy paper in my mind.

I would never again find that perfection in another. I would never again find a love so pure. A love knowing no endless abysses, no jagged rocks, no vipers lurking in the depths of confusion.

A love knowing no confusion.

I became someone else as I stood against the outside rail of the bridge that day. Hours I leaned over that cursed river, the flesh of my arms ripped open and raw by the crumbled concrete and the rusted iron rail I clung to as I stared down at his twisted body. Even though time had stood still, it was only a brief moment, over before I could fully comprehend it. I saw a truth in that moment. I would never know him. Had never really known him, and I had lost him. In one word ... I had lost him, and in that suffocating moment of loss, I realized my own insignificance. The I that was me meant nothing without him, and just when I was about to give up all hope for myself, a sense of detachment moved over me, deadening me to the core. It ran over and through me, flowed beneath my skin, and all of the shame and regret I had at my dismissal of him, was forever altered, also rendered insignificant. I became she, and she felt a cold comfortable consolation in that. She suddenly saw nothing but a corpse.

There was a funeral, of course. *Silk-lined.* They laid him down in the dank earth. *Imprisoned him.* It was so real and yet not real. *In hardened colors,* he was dead. Despite the cacophony of clenched fists, sobs, and wails of mourning. Despite the clap of thunder as the earth hit the hollow depths of his tomb, he would remain dead. There was no release from it. No pardon. No acquittal. It was final. That's all. The gravedigger knew it. His eyes reflected that gruesome truth, honestly and sadly into hers, and even though she has never accepted it, she knew it too.

I took off from the station house on foot, and after a long exhausting walk, I ended up at a café, in a handsome outdoor atrium, sitting amongst the wrought iron tables. Strangers were gorging themselves on expensive wine, lavish food, and idle conversation. *Why do they get to be ignorant? Why do they get to be happy? I hate them.* She was laughing inside. *I hate them. I hate them so much I want to shove the tines of my fork into their eyes.* She felt chewed up and spat out, savage and menacing. I ordered the most expensive unpronounceable dish on the menu, but by the time it arrived, I had lost my appetite and felt like puking, and so I pushed it aside in revulsion and took rather heartedly to drinking my whiskey. Much too much whiskey. After a time, I had trouble lifting the glass from the table, let alone to my mouth, but that and the spectacle I was making of myself didn't stop me from getting on about it with valiant effort.

The bottle under my belt might have numbed my mind, but it couldn't stop the pain in my arms. I stared down at my wrists and forearms. The scars would never heal, and I could still feel the iron spikes of the concrete rail tearing into my flesh even then, opening the wounds afresh, tendons and sinews bare and glistening in the fading light. Forty-two stitches couldn't come close to sealing the wounds. They would weep forever, and I would curse myself over and over again for never really understanding what had happened that day. She was just a child. How could she have possibly understood that the universe had sacrificed him, coldly and without any pity? What purpose could his death have possibly served other than the want for sadistic pleasure? *God won't save us from ourselves.* She was beginning to appreciate that revelation now. The God of our understanding. The God we worship and pray to was created by fools, simply because we are all masochists, every last one of us, living with the blind hope that our suffering will lead us to salvation.

It leads us nowhere.

I paid for my uneaten meal and left the café then. Convinced that my soul was damned, convinced that I would never feel anything ever again, I began sobbing as I made my way down the street, but I kept on walking. The soles of my feet never ceased with their complaints, and I wept and wept and wept all the while as dusk eventually faded into twilight.

I had forgotten a jacket, so I shivered in the cold as the streets closed in around me. Building facades sagged as their shadows melted into the pavement. Shop windows flexed and rippled in the gaslight, and the cracks in the sidewalk opened to giant chasms, seeking to trip my feet. I felt like I might lose my balance, go sprawling face first into the cobblestones at any moment, and I felt feverish. This time I had really done it. I had sunk myself to the bottom of a very dark place, indeed. I decided it was best to take a taxi home.

Folded up into myself from the cold, I waited on the street corner for the next cab. I felt ashamed for wallowing in my own shit that I barely had the courage to look up from the gutter, but when I did, that was when I noticed him, the stranger from the gentleman's pub. He was standing across the street, glaring at me. An urgent desire to flee overcame me, and the utter lack of suitable transport only fueled the terror-stricken hysteria I now found myself consumed by.

I turned to make my escape, but I didn't want to draw attention to myself. I walked quickly. Well, I staggered swiftly like a drunken tart, more or less. I weaved in and down side streets, tottered into various shops, drifted about the aisles, kept my head down and spoke to no one. I felt nervous and fidgety, to the chagrin of the shopkeepers who obviously thought my aim was to commit a felony. But no matter where I turned, he was there, seated at café tables, peering at me through the shop windows, glaring at me from crosswalks. Ahead of me. Behind me. All the time hovering just near enough for me to sense his presence. A whisper in my ear. A shadow hanging just outside my peripheral vision. He seemed a part of me somehow, borne of the tar-drenched rubble beneath my feet, and of all the pain and the lies I had attempted to bury in it. His smile seemed poisoned with loss and regret. A blood red smile, offered only to me. A rose, a dagger, a sacrosanct plea.

It was dark now, and a heavy mist had fallen like an iron curtain over this miserable city, bringing with it the cold, the wind, and the rain. I tried not to pay the weather any mind. It was unseasonably annoying, yes, but it soothed the dangerous drunken fever that I had, intentionally and recklessly, brought upon myself. I kept on walking, crossing, stumbling, and re-crossing the streets. At one point, I lost my left shoe in the gutter and twisted my ankle, and so not by choice, I had to walk more slowly. Maybe my subconscious mind had provoked me to cast that shoe aside. Maybe I had left the laces undone, hoping, shamelessly, that he would gain ground, reach out to me in some way, and end the torment.

I turned onto the square in front of the station house. Its familiarity made me feel safe. It was fiercely lit and overflowing with life. Well, at this late hour, it was more a phantom of life. The dregs and the unwanted. All the hollow corpses of humanity, crawling from pub to pub. As I made my way through the murderously seething mass of drunken death, I saw him again across the street, shoulders down, resolute, persistent, battering his way through the crowd. During a half hour or so, I tried not to, but we looked at each other several times. No more than a hesitant glance. The distance between us always cautiously equal until my car came into view, so I circled back on my own steps, making to come around from another direction with the hope I would lose him in the crowd, but to my astonishment, he had stopped under the street lamp just across from my car.

The rain had begun to fall faster now, harder, sharper on my skin, and the wind had turned colder, lashing at my clothes as if to strip me bare.

And he waited, the faint light of the street lamp falling around him like dismal moonbeams, stretching and drawing his face into a ghostly caricature. The hard lines of his body twisting and turning, as if he were somehow knitted from the mist and all the horrid things that move in the darkness. Rats. Snakes. Slimy back alley shadows. He lowered his chin to his chest, bared his teeth in a coarse smile, and locked his eyes onto mine.

I felt paralyzed with fear and excited at the same time. I didn't know whether to run screaming, to faint, or to charge straight for him like a deranged vengeance-seeking lunatic, but then an idea forced its way through the confusion. I reached for my camera. Its case slung over my arm. Until that moment, I hadn't noticed the weight of it digging into my shoulder.

I drew it out and took aim. He made not the slightest gesture to avoid me. He just stood there, still as stone, staring me down as I snapped off the picture.

"Your soul is mine now, you bastard demon piece of shit," I muttered through shivers and cold wet breath, knowing all the while that it was my soul at stake, not his. "That's right. Your sin is mine now fucker. You have no power here."

I don't know where those words came from, but the spell was potent and comforting. He vanished, and I made a mad, albeit drunken and absurd, dash for my car.

Ever and ever...

Forever.

13

Incipient Delirium

3:00 AM

The traffic lights opposed me at every turn, and the rain chiseled the windscreen, obliterating everything from my view except for the headlights of the oncoming cars. The roads lurched, bowed, and stretched only to come catapulting back at me, biting into the tires and throwing the vehicle into odds with everything.

In light of the ridiculous amount of alcohol coursing through my veins, I was a general menace to public safety. It was a miracle that I made it home unscathed. Yet there I was, drenched and staring at myself in the bathroom mirror, again, like some unhinged derelict, making fit to have a long and rapturous dialog with my other self, my shadow, who more or less ignores me anyway. Just as well, since I have always been ill equipped to deal with revelations of any kind. Having a demon chase you in the streets is quite the revelation, so there I was, all pasty-faced, frizzy-haired, skin dry and sunken in from too much liquor, cigarettes, and not enough real sleep. I hadn't even the strength to contort my face into any emotion other than the blankness that I felt. In that dismal and desperate reflection, a thought came to me, despite my will to ignore it: I would never be anything more than the pathetic creature staring back at me, an imitation of a human being, a tragic pantomime. I took hold of the straight razor and pressed it to the soft skin just under my eye … pressed it with just an adequate amount of force that a tear of crimson emerged and slid down my cheek.

I threw up and then brushed my teeth.

I needed to rest. I needed to get him out of my head, so I pulled the shades, turned off all the lights, including the alarm clock. I even put on some soothing cricket sounds, but sleep would again abandon me. Every muscle in my body was twisted into a coil so tight that I thought my limbs would snap off, so I decided to work.

My darkroom wasn't small, but it appeared that way because it was packed full to overflowing. Developing chemicals sat in jugs on shelves and on the floor. Washbasins shimmered with caustic liquids, and the silhouettes from various bits of machinery and equipment loomed in the half-light at the corners of the room. A safe light hung from the ceiling, casting its diffuse amber glow over everything, but even that couldn't hide the general disarray. The room was as messy and unkempt as I was. I took off my chemical gloves, snapped on the overhead lights, and then I stared at the tatty rope clothesline that hung from wall to ceiling. Suspended from that windblown spider web of confusion was my latest work. My own private night gallery. Every imaginable sin and sentiment was represented, even the most pitiable images of horror and utter despair my tired eyes had ever had the displeasure to encounter, and I couldn't remember any of them. These were not the photographs I had taken over the course of several weeks in the early summer. All the pleasant street scenes had taken on an air of moral abandonment. Nothing but sooty, morbid, licentiousness, virulent filth, and incipient delirium. One photograph in particular, which had once been a mother and daughter triptych at the street corner, had become a nightmarish declaration of oppression and humiliation.

And the little girl just smiled at me…

A burned out hotel room. A child in chains. Blood. Rotting food. Excrement smeared on the floorboards in front of her and on her oh so pretty little dress … the lace now hanging ragged from its hem. A Grandmother clad in leather, spiked choke collar around her neck, cat-o-nine firmly gripped in her hand. *The child's hands are blue.* Little blue tinted hands. Mother is on the bed. So beautiful. Posing for the camera on her hands and knees. Claws tearing at the flesh of her back. A Beast. Tongue lolling. Jaws gaping. Saliva dripping onto mother's bare ass. *Shame. Apathy.* And the child looks off into the distance, teeth filed down into points as she gnaws on a turd and dead rat kabob.

I tore the picture up and threw it to the floor. I had

just imagined it all. Just a play of the light and shadows as I was developing them. I was just tired. Just drunk, and my hands had been shaking with each in turn when I exposed the negatives and then slid them into the developer, but the pictures, they were all the same. The butcher's boy. Axe in hand. Lit cigarette in the other, and the moon shines on, through the storefront window as he stands over a bludgeoned torso. Bloody chunks spatter the walls and the windows. His apron, red. *Hate. Hysteria.* Ribs tear through flesh. Bones a shimmer. Raw hamburger is on sale at the counter.

Then there was burning. Flesh and Fur. White smoke hanging motionless. Grey spirals, unmoving. The lads have had a time of it. Tied the puppy to a post with barbed wire and set it to burn. They stand there. The flames gather. The puppy jerks in the fire while they dance around it, attempting to extinguish the flames with their own urine.

I can't stand what I am feeling. Sweat. Bile in my mouth. I don't know what I'm supposed to be seeing, so I rip all the pictures down from the clothesline and scatter them to the floor. I kick them and step on them. *I will not let fear get the best of me.* I had to make some sense of all this. Was it the liquor? Or could I suddenly see in the darkness, as if the lens of my camera had opened a gateway into some parallel dimension? *No.* Not a dimension. I'd fallen into a pit. A black pit devoid of reason where one could explore the taste for blood and flesh, for rape and for blasphemy. What I saw in those pictures was sin made flesh. Bitter and beautiful. I saw the true essence of humanity. I saw the shadow of the beast that lurks just beneath every innocent smile. I wasn't afraid. I had met that beast before, that day on the bridge, then earlier on the street. Yes, I felt sick, and yes, I was repulsed by the sheer heartlessness and cruelty the photos had exposed, but I was also captivated by their truth. Nothing was blurred. Every emotion was unique and distinct. Sharp, lifelike. The details defined and painfully sublime. Except for the last photograph, which had fallen undamaged at my feet. My dark stranger was there, pixilated and indistinct, gazing up at me as I carried on, having my way with him atop the bar in the gentleman's pub. I couldn't see my own face, didn't recognize my own naked body, but I was sure it was me, my desire, and the longer I stared at that photograph, the more the picture swung wildly in and out of focus. The layers of reality shifting. The glossy surface of the paper began to yellow and crack, etched by a thousand tiny pits and chasms, as did the bar top in the picture. The wood began to splinter and disintegrate into the earth beneath us. Beneath me. Beneath Killy? I could almost feel and smell the soil as my fingers raked and clawed into it. The pub melted away into obscurity, and the street lamps rose upwards, reaching towards the sky. The steel split into gangly gnarled shafts of rusted iron, branching outwards into the ghastly likeness of a barren tree — a Rowan tree — its roots piercing the soil's surface, wrapping thorn-burdened tendrils around the Killy's wrists and ankles, tearing at his flesh. The tree was holding him back, holding him down. *For me.* She wanted it. *I admit it.* She wanted him.

There is this place, a dark place, grimy and wet. A secret and savage place, closed off from the world. We all know this place. Our hearts are darker than we want to admit. We've all taken refuge there from time to time. It's the place where our inner beast shrieks in the moonlight and claws at the walls of our sanity. I had opened the way.

My will was the way…

The room pitched, whirled, and swayed in every possible direction around me, and I felt dizzy, confused. The photograph slipped from my grasp as my knees gave way, and I lost my footing. I fell backwards, crashed to the floor, slammed my head into the steel cupboard behind me. I could taste the blood in my mouth, and then the lights flickered and went out.

IT WAITED FOR YOU THERE,
Right where you had left it.

14

Shattered

October 01, 1998, dark and cold and lonely.

I don't remember getting out of bed. Don't remember getting into bed, either, but somehow, I find myself standing in my bedroom, naked in front of the full-length antique mirror. The silver eroding beneath the chipped glass makes my skin look old and pale, and as I stand there admiring its morbid glow, a foreboding stillness shoots through me. It's as if the grey gloom were condensing around me, shifting its weight, becoming absolutely black — pitch-black — and against the thick of that foul darkness, I can see a sinister figure move into view within the mirror. Its outline broken only by moonbeams shot through the window, and as I step forward towards it, as if to step through that looking glass, all the color in the room completely disappears. A chill settles over my flesh, and everything in that moment seems frozen in time. Even the clock has stopped ticking, held fast by the impenetrable dark.

In the mirror, the demon stands behind me, in reflection only, one ghoulish hand on the back of my neck, the other moving across my hips and stomach. Slow. Slowly moving down to the bare cleft between my legs, and then, he's inside of me. Long, slender, frightfully cold fingers, reaching into what is now an open wound. I let loose a moan, which crystallizes and diminishes into the frigid night air, but he says nothing as his hand leaves my neck to clamp down over my mouth. I can feel the jagged edges of his fingernails pressing into my cheek. I reach for the mirror. If I could somehow touch it, I feel certain that the illusion will vanish and with it, the horrible desire I feel surging within me, but when I do put my fingers to it, the surface ripples and flexes at the pressure, and then my arm passes through the glass all the way to my elbow. It flexes violently, once more, then shatters into a million pieces, sending shards of glass flying in every direction like shooting stars in the moonlight.

Cutting into my face, they hit me as if a bomb exploded, slashing at the tender skin of my breasts and lacerating my arms and legs. The demon's image shudders behind me, and a stale, rancid gust of air fills the room. He pushes me forward, doubling me over myself. I can see the diffuse outline of leathery wings spreading out, eclipsing the floor beneath my feet. I feel his hair on my back, the rush of it against my skin, and almost with pleasure, I know there is no escaping my fate. I bite into my lip so hard that I taste blood. My knees weaken, but he holds me firm, tells me to close my eyes. I know what's coming. Had felt it so often with Killy. When the first blow strikes, it strikes with precision, with more following, faster and faster. I struggle against them, not to escape the punishment, not to merely endure it, but to take the pain in deeper, so deep that it blacks out the world. When I think of it, the silence in that pain, I begin to cry, but the worst of it … the worst of my fears is that they are tears of joy and surrender. A release from the agony of nothingness I feel inside. A release from my own anger and hatred. I've wanted that release so badly for so long, I can't ever remember being without that want, and as I feel him clawing at my soul, I feel not the sharp searing pain of innocence lost, but only the warm flood of absolution cascading down between my legs. I can feel a blackness deepening within me as his thrust becomes more determined, more exacting, and I force myself back against him, crying out as an ecstasy only death can know washes over me. I want to turn and face him. I want to embrace him, declare that I love him, and offer myself to him in servitude. I can't stop crying, begging, wanting. His hands, his hatred, moving over and through me, hungry, desperate, tracing blood up along my stomach with his fingertips. My blood. The crimson stain of my hollow. I feel his teeth press against my flesh again, and then everything stops. Moonbeams seize the floor and freeze it into a shimmering sheet of ice. The ebb and flow of time falters, and I fall into his shadow. "Rowan," he says, "do not weep for your wounds. What's done is done. The sin becomes you, don't you see? Its regret stains and colors your blood. It's the hate in your blood that I desire. Beneath the flesh, you and I are already one. *Your blood and mine.* Demons come in many forms, Rowan. You know what to do. Dance, Rowan. You must dance."

In those words, I lost all knowledge of myself. Lost all comprehension of death and divinity. *I'm ready now.* He knows this, and in an instant, he firmly grips the back of my neck and forces me to the floor. My body limp, knees buckling as they hit the bare wood, the glass from the mirror cuts through to pierce cartilage and bone; yet, of the pain, I still feel nothing…

Barely able to breath, I woke up to a shattered mirror, and I felt that any small shred of sanity I might have been able to hold onto had also been shattered. For the first time, I actually felt fear. I had felt fear in my dreams before, what I thought was real fear, but now I know what fear is, and I was repulsed by how much I had savored it.

Dawn had just broken, and a filthy dirty light tore through those god-awful ragged drapes. Above me, the empty space of the ceiling seemed more vast than I ever remembered, its blank comfort completely foreign to me now, so I got up. I don't know how I managed, as my bruised and bloodied body felt as if I had endured one hundred and twenty days of Sodom, but I got up anyway, and then I carelessly traversed the sea of glass on my way to the bathroom, leaving bloodied footsteps in my wake.

I could barely stand but for the sink holding me upright. I turned on the tap and shoveled handfuls of cool water into my mouth, splashing a little over my face and chest in the process. I looked at myself in the mirror, again. I looked haggard, flushed, burning with fever, and I felt a strong urge to throw up. After a few minutes, I vomited all over myself, blood mostly, and possibly partly digested chunks of my soul.

After vomiting, I made my way through the debris and crawled back into bed. I felt some relief, but I knew it wouldn't be long before the nausea would return like a death throe. I started shivering, and my knees, caked with blood and glass, ached unbearably.

I wanted to die. The bed sheets offered little comfort, and I could find no relief for all my fitful tossing and turning. Eventually, I sank back into a dreadful kind of sleep. A half sleep, with one hand over my eyes and one foot in the grave. *The shadows are on the move.* I can feel them, taunting me, twisting the already tattered fabric of my mind, tearing it at the seams, unraveling the fibers one by one. My life is falling to pieces … like those fucking god-forsaken drapes.

15

Translucency

October 02, 1998 … it's a sickness.

O ver the next few days. I took to the streets. Festering wounds on my knees and heavy with fever, I took to dragging my limp and disheveled catastrophe of a body around town. I looked a fright. My tatty thrift store clothes hung loose on my bones; I couldn't staunch the bleeding; and my pants were a mess, coated at the knees with a combination of dried and fresh blood. I hadn't even showered or washed my hair. Whatever had decided to cling to me was beyond the liberation of soap and water.

So there I was, wandering, and I didn't know why. Maybe it was an asinine attempt to reconnect with normalcy, to blend in with the ordinary. I never liked browsing the town, hated the insufferable closeness of it all. You almost become invisible, just another shifting wraith in the crowd. People bump into you, but they look straight through you and don't pay you any mind whatsoever, not even enough for a polite apology because they almost knocked you down.

Nobody really looked at me, and if they did, it was to steer their children away from me, but mostly, nobody took even a fleeting notice of anything beyond themselves or the odd trinkets they happened to be obsessed with at the moment. I've never minded being reduced to minutiae. Never minded being ignored. *I've always felt alone.* No one had actually recoiled from me, or smirked at me, or accosted me in any way, but I still felt like a plague victim. Like the ordinary knew I was not of their kind. That I was contaminated. They could see it in me, could sense it all around me. I stunk of death. I was not fit for polite normal society. The things that I have seen have marked me and left me for dead. People don't really want to see what lurks in the shadows. I've looked, and what I've seen shines on in my eyes. No one wants to stare into that reflection. I don't belong with these nice, proper people. I don't belong here or anywhere now.

I don't belong.

As I trudged along, I sank farther and farther into those feelings of despair and isolation, and yet I felt free. I don't think I was fooling myself in this. I felt detached from the expected and the accepted. I felt indifferent to hope and meaning, and that, to me, smacked of freedom. In every reflective surface I passed, the faces of the dead stared back at me, but there was glass between us, an endless translucency between us. They were just images blurred by the glare of life, no real substance, their faces stretched, mouths agape, their glazed half-lidded eyes barely concealing their hunger, their wantonness, their lust, and their greed. Their flesh had been torn from their bones, their bodies violated, and they wept, not for their own salvation but for mine. Their suicide was my rebirth, and yet I could barely look at them. I couldn't feel them. Couldn't touch them, or smell them. They couldn't harm me. They were trapped, mere apparitions reflected off a lens, and I was free, alive, and angry, so I wandered around some more. Day after day. I stopped into pubs, fancy bistros, and cafés. I sipped, chewed, and spit it all back out again. I wandered into shops, made nonsensical and needless purchases. Shoelaces. I bought hundreds of pairs of shoelaces in every imaginable color, shape, and size. I tied them to my wrists, twisted them through my hair, braided them around my neck, slipped them over doorknobs, and hung them from the drapery rods — knotted, bowed, and knotted thrice again.

I frequented tattoo shops in an attempt to cover my body with astrological symbols, alchemical incantations, and endless talismanic glyphs with the hopes of protecting myself from the vile and despicable images, words, and thoughts that now continuously assaulted my mind. The pain of the needle released me in some way, turned my inwardness outward. It was much more than a violation of the flesh. It wasn't vague like that. Its reach was far more penetrating, far beyond the flesh. Its sharpness cut through all of my barriers, allowing all the empty years and the agony of them to rise to the surface, to exist in a reality outside of my subconscious. I could finally see and feel the blasphemous beast who tore at my shadow. Shame was the name it whispered to itself in the darkness, and for the first time in my life, I could actually know that which had escaped me for what seemed an eternity.

During those two days, I kept my head down, tried to make eye contact with as few people as possible, and when my eyes did happen to inadvertently catch the attention of another's, it was only rage that I felt. You see, I didn't actually need the camera anymore. Everyone's sin was tattooed to their soul, and I could see everything, beyond the flesh, behind even the coldest eyes. It was completely out of my control. I just started doing it, as if I had always possessed this … this sin eating gift. Maybe I always had, and I just couldn't remember. Maybe the act of my seeing them for who they really were released them in some way.

I had lunch with Cameron. As usual, he was a huge ball of tension, pure energy with no emotional core, and it propelled him blissfully through the days. How I envied him.

"Rowan, you look like hammered shit," he said to me, and even though I hadn't looked in the mirror in days, I had no grounds to argue with him. Knocking back his pint as if he were trying to wash the sight of me from his mind like a bad taste, he ranted on and on about how the department was worried about me along with other idle chatter and gossip.

I found it difficult to keep my attention focused on him enough to absorb anything he was saying. Something about a hideous triple murder suicide. Severe mutilation and necrophilia. *I'm slipping away.* I tried to focus on his words. Did he really say necrophilia? The words just flew through the air, separating, rearranging themselves into hideous acronyms and demented *Mad Libs*. Yes, Cameron was a cannibal too. He talked relentlessly, effortlessly. *Wounds. Those words were gaping wounds.* He fed on the words, fed on their horrific imagery, and all I could do was look intently at the stale, decrepit yellow corpse of the Canelé on my plate, which I had massacred with my plastic fork without cause.

It's a crying shame to sacrifice good pastry.

Other than that, no one bothered me. No one called me, but then again, I left my mobile turned off. No one except Killy made any attempt to find me or question me as to why I had not shown up for work or my scheduled therapy sessions. Of course, I could have made a grand appearance, for appearance' sake. I could have poked at the cancerous tumor and given myself a chronic migraine too, or I could have sent my stomach into fits and spasms for no real reason, but frankly, what was the point?

My existence was pointless.

Not to mention that the rather craptacular state of my physical being would have repulsed even those with a strong stomach. The stench of my body was enough to nauseate me, and I had grown accustomed to it. It was just better for everyone if I stayed out of sight, so I rose late and barely ate. I felt starved, and yet the starvation felt cleansing. I began falling into what might only be described as a self-inflicted coma. I felt like I was slowly sinking into a violent flood of random particles. My world had slipped into a layer of transparency, the ideal image of me clinging to one side, particles of filth and dust clinging to the other. This was my new and improved reality, so I decided in a fit of reckless abandon that I would do a bit of redecorating. I went home and drank myself into a ridiculous state, and then, taking staggering, unsteady steps, I proceeded to ransack my flat.

Hour after hour, all the remainder of the afternoon, swinging wood-splintered and nailed-gouged arms with jerky, incoherent movements, I flung myself about the place, knocking furniture over, rendering to dust all the idle, meaningless trinkets I had collected over the years, and smashing all the lamps to bits.

It wasn't liquor-induced hysteria that I had surrendered to. I just wanted an empty dark room. Was that too much to ask? I didn't think so, and so I tore up the floorboards, ripped all the draperies from the windows, and nailed up the planks of wood in their place. Not so much as a sliver of dawn would breach my fortress.

No light … No shadows.

Sometimes the muffled sound of a gust of wind battered against the fortifications, but it had no means to hurt me, and that was my only consolation. I felt the tyranny of my own shadow. It follows me around, smug, silent, deliberately ignorant of me, but ever present, poking and prodding at my soul with an insufferable stick of despair. I was so tired. I don't think I had ever felt so tired. It was as if the slightest particle of dust in motion might set me off my feet and cast me away, spiraling into nothingness.

I collapsed to the floor, rolled over onto my back, lit a cigarette, and smoked it. And then I lit another, and another, and another as I watched the ceiling slide down the walls to crush me, inch by inch, hoping I wouldn't notice until it was too late. As dusk moved in, and the little pinholes of light through the wooden planks disappeared, the nicotine drenched haze clouding the room stirred like the mid-morning fog. Breaching even the minutest void, it filled in the ruptured spaces, and, for what it's worth, its stale cat piss stench gave me a tortured sort of peace.

I spent endless weeks in this new and astonishing darkness. So much so that I took to wearing sunglasses on cloudy days. The meager light hurt my eyes even then.

Many a night, in the depthless distance of eve's hallow, when the day's long spent and the dawn seems an eternity away, around three a.m., the witching hour, when all sleeps except for the shifting tremors that move in the darkness, I could feel my shadow rise to the surface, rise up from the pit of my soul. I was convinced that it was the disembodied lament of the abyss, deepening within me. I liked to think it was that, for I had nothing to fear from my shadow. It had been with me for as long as I could remember. It had whispered to me in secret at my darkest hour, that day on the bridge, when I first heard its voice.

While wallowing in the chaos of my life, I've come to know one true thing. I have seen the world. I have seen the demons. Formless. Timeless. Faith in absentia. I have seen absolute darkness. This is the only reality, the only truth I know. I feel as if I am just beginning to see a faint glimpse of the future. The real future. The end of days. I'm not getting it in any finite detail, but it is perceptible even in the dim light. I can see the action, the reaction, and the consequence, and I have become dreadfully aware of everything around me. I've always feared that someday I might be plagued by madness. It happens often enough in my profession, but I don't think this is madness. One cannot be self-aware and mad at the same time. Can a madman know they're mad?

It's not madness.

It's just a sharpening of the senses — a second sight.

Or maybe I am just lying to myself, I don't know.

Maybe I am just suffering from exhaustion. *No.* I'm a despicable vile thing. I hate humanity, and I have the world to thank for that. I want to stab it and kill it for ruining me, for ruining every corpse I've ever had the unfortunate pleasure to set my eyes on. They never catch the killers. Maybe only killers can see killers?

Maybe I'm a killer.

I don't know what I am capable of doing. To anyone. To myself. I don't really know myself anymore, or if this newfound power and rage within me is simply a grotesque manifestation of my corrupted innocence. Regardless of what it is though, I fear that I might lose it as miraculously as I found it, and that I will be powerless to stop it and lost without it. I feel stronger than I ever have. I don't want to be weak anymore. When one feels powerless, an impoverished soul will seek comfort where it can, will cling to anything within its grasp, but none of this matters anymore. I can feel destiny snapping and snarling at my door, and I have no will left to fight it.

I don't want to fight it.

I don't want to fight anything anymore, so I finally acquiesced and accepted a call from Killy. He had very insistently argued that we needed to talk. I have nothing to say worth any weight, and the thought of his flesh against mine makes me want to gnash my teeth over rusted nails, but I agreed to meet him back at his flat at noon. Whatever is going to happen, there is nothing to be done about it. Nothing I care to do about it?

I felt nervous and angry that I was being forced to leave my dark room, so I walked for about an hour or so. The roads went on and on infinitely in an unbroken stretch of shameless consumerism, decadence, and deceit. There was absolutely no wind, and it seemed cold, as cold as all of the faces swapping currency for comforts and cages. When I arrived at his flat, I found all the drapes drawn, and Killy, lying naked in the middle of the bed with his arms flung out wide, calla lilies across his chest. *He loved death lilies, not me. It's never about me.* He looked smug with anticipation, then, frustrated and resentful like a naughty little child, probably a reaction to the expression of disgust on my face, as if the sex-starved body he had been hoping to offer me as a bribe for my affection — for the surrender of my soul — had somehow transformed itself into a maggot-riddled corpse.

It had, and I felt like puking just looking at him, so I started the one-sided dialog with a, "Well now, Killy, what have we here? Is this your idea of an invitation, or should I just slit my wrists now and grovel at your feet?"

Grovel is such a hostile word, so I had deliberately pronounced each syllable with the malice it deserved, but Killy isn't so easy to taunt. He's always held his emotions in a constant state of restraint. He is a master at self-control, and that is where he had always had the greatest advantage over me. *Tricky, tricky little dicky.* Charm and cleverness had always worked for him, had always gotten him exactly what he was after. I had no defense against his will. Until now, all I had at my disposal were cheap jibes, sarcastic witticisms, and second-rate humiliating remarks, devoid of any insight, mystical illumination, or clarity, and he mocked me for it. He used me, and I let him. He never really saw me. He only saw what he could possess. What he could manipulate and abuse. It's different now. I know it, but he doesn't, and that was my advantage. I had some clever of my own now. *Who needs charm?* I had harnessed the power of my shadow. I had embraced hate, had drunk it in through my pores. When you find your world falling to pieces all around you. When the lies you told yourself become ugly truths. When your insecurities about yourself become the things you fear the most, everyone desires to act on their hate. Murder fantasies, death fantasies, rape fantasies. Fantasies that seemed so unreal and so unnatural we'd never ever admit them to anyone, not even a Priest. That is until they start pushing at you. If you could say anything, do anything, *what would you do?*

I know. They're not just fantasies. They are lies. Elaborate in their span and dimension, intricate in their intrigues. Lies absolve us. Lies dull the pain, and allow us to live in ignorant bliss. We can imagine killing someone, and we feel better, but we don't kill them, so it's a lie. I wish I had such fantasies, but I don't. Never have had. I have only my nightmares: chaotic nursery rhymes sung to me in blackened tongues. Killy is one of those nightmares. He lives vicariously through his own demented fantasies, and it's about time I had one of my own. When he asks me to take off my clothes and join him, I don't answer him. I can't answer him. No words come to mind, because I can see his lie spread out before me. I feel cold and dark and empty inside when I'm with him. I have never felt love. Love is happiness, but only if you believe in it. Most times, it too turns out to be a lie, just another of those fantasies. I loved Rhys, but that couldn't save him. Couldn't save him from poverty, or from the abuses of his father, or from the cold indifference of his mother. It couldn't even save him from the treachery of his own rotted and lost soul. My stupid naive response to his plea that day — no better than the vehement sting of discipline — had forced all of those blades in a little deeper. I should have just said yes. *Had all his hope for a better life rested with me?* Now, looking back, I don't believe he ever had any hope. He never saw the inexplicable wonder that I saw when I looked into his eyes, nor did he feel the touch of a miracle when our lips pressed together in innocence. He never felt the poetry of his own soul the way I did. My love couldn't change that, not then, not now, not ever. *Rhys, my soul would lament for you if it could only feel something, anything at all.*

Even that's rubbish really. All of it. What's the use in having such knowledge of love when that knowledge only brings sorrow, humiliation, and defeat? Love. It's just a useless fickle fantasy. A fairy tale so repugnant, so damaging, and so mortally wounding, it's not worth a bucket of piss. Ironically, at least Killy and I both agreed on something: Love is a lie. We can choose to fall, base before its treachery. We can allow its obsessive desires to consume us, to change us, to weaken our resolve and torture our souls. Yes, we can choose that … if we must. On the other hand, we can choose salvation and reject the lie. I can choose to reject it, reject the dark truths about love that I cannot accept.

The choice is and always has been mine.

I wish I didn't know such things. I wish I couldn't see Killy's love for the despicable self-serving thing that it was. I wish I didn't know the inevitable, and I wish I didn't know the choice I had already made, but I do.

It all happened so quickly. In a moment, all Killy's elegant deceitful grace turned into idiotic astonishment. For the first time, I could see fear in his eyes, and that made me smile.

16

The End is The End, *nothing more, nothing less*

October 31, 3:00 AM … Wounds, the words are open wounds.

I understand those words so very clearly, for the first time in my life. Death dreamt us all, and it's calling out to me. Its sweetly scented breath whispers my name. I feel fulfilled. I feel accepted. No longer does my shadow ignore me. No longer am I a stranger to myself, so I stabbed him. I stabbed and stabbed and stabbed at the corpse beneath me. I had always loved Killy's body, slender but strangely powerful. His skin just glowing in the silvery light of the moon as it stole like a specter through the window, negating all color and emotion and time. I stabbed him while he lay there, calm on the bed. His body like cold hard porcelain against the backs of my thighs. He didn't fight when I grasped his arms at the elbows and pushed them up over his head. He didn't say a word when I kissed his neck or when I pressed my breasts against him. He was such a tease, but I had long ago grown tired of his idle taunts and threats. The salvation of my soul lay in his capacity for love, and I would cut it out of him if I had to.

"Beg," I whispered in his ear.

I wanted to hear him submit. I needed it. My black heart could subsist no longer without the validation. I demanded a confession, demanded ablutions in tears and in blood. I deserved release. He could no longer deny me that, and so he did … beg. Eventually. He begged blindly, breathlessly, and desperately, without reservation or objection because he didn't know what he was begging for. He thought he knew. He always thought he knew everything, the arrogant fuck. I knew he assumed that he had judged the situation accurately, but vanity and pride would betray him now. His narcissistic charm reflected nothing but the fool that he was.

I leaned back, reaching for the foot of the bed, reaching for the blade that I had hidden there, like a secret, and then I stabbed him. His skin started going cold almost immediately. His breath, quicker in pace. He almost sounded satisfied, and it angered me. Could he take what I had to offer? *Would he suffer for once?* Would he cry out in torment or scream with desire? Either way, it was too late, and I couldn't even pretend to care. I had held onto that bridge until I was numb and bloodied. I had spent an eternity trying to tell myself just to hold on. *Wasted eternity.* My shadow was telling me now to let go, and for the first time in my life, I wanted to. I would take what I desired from this creature lying beneath me. He was all mine to enjoy as I pleased. He had no power over me anymore, no will to deny me. How I adored the hate I felt for him, adored the sickening rawness of it. I wanted to cut him. I wanted to disembowel him and chew on his sin.

So I stabbed him again, the blade dancing across his flesh, digging in one moment and then offering cool respite the next. There is nothing like the liberation one feels when the limits of one's endurance are tested, and he was going to be tested. AGAIN … as he struggled against it … AND AGAIN … as he surrendered to it … AGAIN … as he wept … until his adoration for me flowed freely. I stabbed him one last time, but he had nothing left to give. The illusionist had finally been revealed. His tricks and trinkets were nothing but foolish diversion. What I wanted had slicked down and pooled onto the bed, an offering steeped in sincerity and selflessness. A sacrifice. It was all I had ever wanted from him, and I felt faint. All the blood was driving me out of my mind. My skin felt hot and prickly. I wanted him to look at me, to face me — to face the demon fate had created — but when I looked upon his face, his eyes were no longer dark and empty. There was light in them, but just as I had always suspected, there was nothing in that light. There were no sweet sentiments, no tender comforts. Nothing. A bitter, empty nothing, so I cried out. Shouted out my testimony, my confession, and it echoed back from the hollow.

How temperate the still waters of desire.
How filthy the stain.
Ripping and tearing into my flesh,
How luxurious and inevitable the pain.

I could taste iron and death in the air, and I wanted him so much, much more than I ever intended. Even in death, he was trying to tempt me with his poison. Trying to deceive me yet again. Take advantage of me. Lure me with vile seductions: his mouth, his hands, his cock. *Like he did to all those others.* I stabbed him again. *I had no other choice.* I had allowed his hatred into my heart, and I felt nothing but cold sweat — the sheets and my body, soaked through to the bone with it. *What's happening to me?* I see black water. I see phantoms, slithering across the breach. Ashen skies falling all around me in haunted memories. *A thousand liquid memories, clinging desperately to my soul.* My poor rotted soul. *Dead thing. Evil thing. Vile thing.* I left it there, filthy viscous thing that it was.

SNAP!

My hands are cold. Cold steel in my hands. Cold steel and blood. *Too much blood on my hands.* Glistening, liquid ebony in the fell light from the window. *Sad blackened shafts of light cutting through the silence.* Cutting across the moon.

THAT DEMON MOON.

It mocks me. Its treachery scents the mist with rancid tears, rot, and sorrow. That dread melancholy moon. In the half-light, it blushes and blooms. Clinging to the night sky, shining down upon our empty tombs.

SNAP!

I feel the demon, writhing beneath me. I feel its lies like daggers. Even its tears are lies. A plea for mercy, lost to the wind. Nothing but a whisper. No more than the whisper of subterfuge and sin. *Burnt offerings, it says.* And the blood flows. The blood is the life. The blood is the only life there is.

SNAP!

"Rowan, please … no—"

I tremble at the sound. I tremble at the dull, gurgling insignificant sound of his voice.

SNAP!

My will is the way. The dark is coming, and a mystic wind. Lie down now, my love. Lie still and silent upon the dark waters. Where all the lost souls come to drown. Their screams die away upon still black waters, and the dead surround me.

Be silent.

Be still.

Grey tombstones, buried in the cold dank earth, and the blood flows into the silence, the stillness, and the night. *I have been deceived.* I'm sinking deeper. Innocence is lost to me. All I can see is darkness and doom in my dreams. I no longer doubt it.

SNAP!

I no longer doubt my own screams.

June 18, 1975

To My Beloved Rhys

I dreamt…yes.
I felt…yes.
I breathed…yes.
With my whole heart and soul,
I wanted…yes.
But it was too cold
Too cold and lonely for you
To hear me.

Cheryl Anne Gardner is a writer of dark, often disturbing art-house novellas and abstract flash fiction. Her love of literature began at an early age with Bram Stoker's Dracula. Captivated by the Gothic and Dark Romantic stylings of Poe, Lovecraft, Kafka, and de Sade, her passion for the macabre manifests itself throughout her own work to this day, and she pays homage often where she can. She lives with her husband and ferrets on the east coast USA, is an enthusiastic gardener, and her flash fiction has been published at Dustbin, The Menacing Hedge, Pure Slush, Danse Macabre, The Carnage Conservatory, Negative Suck, and at The Molotov Cocktail among others. When she isn't writing, she likes to chase marbles on a glass floor, eat lint, play with sharp objects, and make taxidermy dioramas with dead flies.

You can find more of her work at Twisted Knickers Publications and at various online retailers.

Titles by Cheryl Anne Gardner

The Kissing Room
The Thin Wall
The Splendor of Antiquity
Logos
And Death Dreamt Us All